Foundation of Doubt

Foundation of Doubt

Nadine Burr

Library of Congress Control Number:		2024921776
ISBN:	Hardcover	979-8-3694-3189-4
	Softcover	979-8-3694-3190-0
	eBook	979-8-3694-3191-7

Print information available on the last page.

Rev. date: 10/18/2024

To order additional copies of this book, contact:
Xlibris
844-714-8691
www.Xlibris.com
Orders@Xlibris.com
862256

Dedication

I dedicate this book to all the men and women out there looking for love, searching for the special someone.

I dedicate this book to women and men who are looking for themselves.

I dedicate this book to the sisters in the struggle, trying to raise their families on their own,

I dedicate this book to my sisters in Christ. The power is within.

The foundation is only as strong as the love that you share with one another but you must first be true to yourself, first love yourself, first take care of yourself, so that you can care for others

When you give love you receive love, god bless you all.

Acknowledgement

There are so many I would like to thank for the process of this book but first, THANK YOU FATHER GOD for giving me the courage and the strength to put what's in my mind and in my heart on these pages, along with all the other projects I had going on. I would not have been able to do it without you, Lord you were there every step of the way as always.

I would also like to say THANK YOU to my children. You were all there when I needed you as always mommy love you so much.

THANKYOU to the XLIBRIS team and Publishing Company, your expertise, patience, and dedication are exceptional. I would like to give a HUGE special THANK YOU to Daryl Yap, Senior Marketing Consultant, it got a little crazy there for a minute, Thank so much for your patience and advice.

Last but not least, I would like to thank my sister in Christ Deborah Alexander for her inspirations and affirmations that I would never forget, and if I'm forgetting anyone, blame it to my head and not my heart, I love you all. God bless.

Nadine Burr

Prologue

‘Tish was able to maintain an addiction, through credit which was the worst mistake she could’ve ever made in her life. That mistake put her and her family in jeopardy. Tish was a functional user, maintaining her household and her family, her husband Darian had no idea that she was back to using once she became clean before they were married. No one knew what Tish was doing, not even her sister who mysteriously disappeared while looking for Tish, but things really turned for the worst when Tish found letters from Darien’s past relationship.

Chapter 1

Frustrated and confused, Darien quickly jumped out of the moving car while Dutch was trying to park. He slammed the door shut and hurried into National Bank to use the ATM machine as he had. He punched the keys with blood-soaked fingers. He thought about his wife and two daughters being held up by some well-known neighborhood thugs. The frustration started building up even more as the receipts kept popping out without the cash, one after another read declined, declined, declined. He began to kick the machine. He knew there was an error somewhere, but he didn't have time for this. The life of his family was at stake, and he was praying they were still alive. He hit the machine as hard as he could, leaving splashes of blood on the glass.

Just as Darien turned away to walk out of the bank, he caught movement out the corner of his eye, a bill dropping. He stared down at the $20 bill just lying there, staring back at him. Suddenly, bills started coming out of the machine one after another like running water, $20 bills flying so fast they started dropping to the floor. Without a second thought of the consequences, he began stuffing them into his pockets, socks, and jacket sleeves. Sweat began to pour down his face as he ran out of the bank. Checking his surroundings, he swung the door open and jumped in the car, trying to gain his composure. Dutch, Darien, his best friend from high school, looked at him like he had just lost his mind. With the money balled up in his hand and a look on his face, Darien told Dutch to step on the gas and get the hell out of there. Dutch, trying to keep his eye on the road, and on Darien as he pulls money out of his socks to stuff inside his pockets.

It's about 3:30 PM, and gangs of schoolchildren are on their way home. They constantly examine their surroundings as the car sits idle at the light. The light changes, and the children chat with each other while slowly walking across the street when Dutch suddenly pressed down on the horn and Darien motions for him to stop.

"Man, you blowin' at the kids, do you see her standing there? Damn man, you just bringing attention to us," he said while pointing at the crossing guard. Dutch, a 37-year-old, five-foot-nine brown-skinned man with a slim stature, never thought they would make it out of the intersection before the light changed. Overwhelmed with nervousness, Darien looked over at Dutch, "Look man you take this money down to the Big M club and wait for me there, I'll explain everything to you later and I promise you, if those thugs lay one hand on my family, they're dead."

"They are not that stupid."

"Dutch. Yes, they are, because they will do anything for money. Let me out, I'll walk in the block and hurry away from here. It might be swarming with cops in a minute."

Dutch leaned over and looked out the car window at Darien, "Tell me what the hell just happened back there."

"I said later... I have to get back to Tish," Darien pushed his way through the door just in time to see the man who used to be his best friend, hand on his wife's breast. Darien charged at him with the thought of murder on his mind. He wrapped his arms around his neck, trembling as he tightened harder and harder. Tish screamed for Darien to let him go, she just knew he was going to kill him. All Darien was waiting to hear was bones crushing, and he wasn't going to stop until he did. His grip got tighter and tighter.

Sweat poured from his face. It was only the sound of guns clicking and the voice of someone saying that he would put a bullet through this little princess's head that made Darien loosen his deadly grip. Rattle fell to the floor, coughing and gasping for air while Darien ran over to his daughter.

"If any one of you did anything to hurt my family, I swear I will come after each, and every one of you," said Darien, with hate and tears in his eyes.

"You ain't in no position to make threats, my friend, just hand over what you owe me and we're out of here."

"I never owed you anything, never. I don't even know what you're talking about," said Darien staring at the money on the floor. When the guys bent down to pick it up, he kicked one of them. They turned around and hit Darien so hard that he flew back against the wall and hit the floor. The others started laughing and pointed the guns towards Darien as they picked the rest of the money up. Darien looks Tish in the eyes.

"You okay, Tish?" he asked while scanning her up and down, making sure she wasn't harmed in any way. He looked around and noticed how much of a mess the house was from the struggles. When they first came to the house, there were just too many of them, and he hated to leave his family like that. Darien swore to get them all back one at a time, one day. The guy that Darien kicked swung off and punched him in the mouth on his way out the door.

"That's for earlier nigga, do not try that shit again, 'ya hear?" Darien just sat there. He realized he had to think about what would happen to Tish and the girls while he was fighting with these guys. He just felt helpless and all alone when they left, Darien hugged his family.

"I do not know what I would have done if my babies were hurt," he cried. "I love my baby so much I will kill for you if I have to" Tish got up and locked the door then headed back to Darien. She reached for a box of Kleenex and tried to clean his face. He pushed her hand away.

"It hurts too bad baby," he said. "Wait a while please." She nodded.

His 10-year-old daughter, Shakima, put her arms around his neck, "Daddy I was not afraid, I knew you were coming back to save us."

"Yes baby," Darien reassured. "Do you know your daddy right? I love you sweetie." He put his forehead to hers and kissed her on the nose.

"I love you too Daddy," she said in a soft voice. His seven-year-old, Rahanna, stayed close to Tish, holding onto her leg. Darien reached for her and put her on his lap.

"Is my princess okay?" he asked, as he carefully searched her over from head to toe.

"I was scared, Daddy. The men hurt you," Rahanna cried.

"No, they didn't baby they didn't hurt me. I wouldn't let them hurt you or me sweetness or any one of us. I'm fine I'm not afraid of those bad guys and I do not want you to be afraid they're not coming back here anymore." Darien continued to hold her.

"Okay," she nodded. Darien looked around the room and shook his head. He couldn't believe how quickly the place got messed up like that. He turned around and looked at the girls,

"I need you girls to help mommy clean this mess up. Go ahead and get started and she will join you in a minute. I need to talk with her, alright?"

"Okay Daddy," says Shakima. She grabbed her sister's hand and walked to the center of the room and glanced around with a confused look on her face, wondering where to start.

Darien slowly rose from the sofa, took Tish by the hand, and stood her up in front of him, "Baby we're out of here, I'm tired of these punks thinking they can just take over people's shit and demand something. Ripping people off, scaring children, punk asses thought they were ripping me off for my last money, but I have a trick for them."

Tish started crying and covering her face. She couldn't bear to look at Darien when she told him the horrible truth that caused all this drama, *Darien is one of the nicest men you could ever meet,* she thought, *and a lot of people are crazy about him, especially his friends, but he can have a temper that you wouldn't believe.* She removed her hands from her face and looked him in the eyes. "Honey it was not a rip-off. I owed them the money," she said sobbing. "I'm so sorry Darien. I'm sorry I took you all through this. It's all my fault you could've been killed. The girls could've been killed." She fell back onto the sofa and buried her head in her lap.

'What do you mean Tish?" Darien asked. "What are you talking about?"

She looked at him, "I needed a little something from them and I couldn't pay for it at the time so I promised them that I would give them the money today. I had no idea it was going to turn out like this."

"Baby you've been clean for a long time, it's been years, why? Why now?" He asked. "You haven't used anything since way before the girls was born." Tish didn't want to tell Darien about his sister's friend Tonya, and that she knew what was going on between them. One reason was because she had no proof, and Darien always told her if you accuse someone of something, be able to put your hands on them and say I *got you.* She couldn't cope with the fact that he was spending so much time at his sister's house instead of at home. There was a time when Darien would always be around Tish. They did everything together and talked on the phone for hours when they weren't around each other. People would tell them that they had the perfect relationship, and they spent so much time together that they started to look like one another. Those were the days that Tish missed and wanted back. They started drifting apart when Darien's sister's girlfriend came and started hanging around her all the time. Tish turned back to drugs to replace the emptiness. She fell, not having Darien at home.

"Darien, I was bored out of my mind being at home. Just me and the girls all the time, and when you did come home, it was just time to go to bed. We would have a chance to have dinner together but most of the time we couldn't. Baby, I was really lonely but-"

"Why this Tish, you could've talked to me about it."

"Darien, I know the first thing that would've come out of your mouth was that I was overreacting, being jealous, and I didn't have anything to worry about. I didn't want to hear those words again." Tish exclaimed.

Darien sat down next to her on the sofa, "Girls go to your room so I can talk to mommy for a while, okay?" he said. They waited and watched the girls as they walked away and resumed talking.

"Tish," he said as he looked, trying to search for the truth. He was not satisfied with the reason she just gave him. "There's no way in hell you started back using just because I wasn't home." He was yelling at this point. "You've got to come better than that because I'm not buying it. I'm going to find out what it is before this night is over and you will definitely talk then."

"If that's what you really want then why can't you just believe what I tell you, Darien?"

"Because I know it's not the truth Tish!"

She got up from the sofa and headed for the kitchen. Darien grabbed her by the arm and pulled her back down, 'Where do you think you're going? I'm talking to you."

"Darien, let my arm go you're hurting me," Tish gasped.

"Not until you tell me the truth. I want to know what's going on with you. I cannot leave you here in this house with the girls knowing that something is bothering you so much that you have to start using again. I do not want what happened today to ever happen again, do you understand what I'm telling you?"

"It's Tonya, Darien, I'm telling you it's Tonya." Tish admitted. "Who?" he yelled.

"Tonya. I think you've been spending too much time with her and not being at home with your family."

"What the heck she got to do with this?"

"She's keeping you away from us, Darien, and I know she is."

Darien couldn't believe what he was hearing. Though he always had a crush on Tonya since childhood and he did enjoy her company, he had no intention of leaving his family, "Honey, Tonya does not have anything on you. I love you and the girls. You don't have to worry about that."

"You are there with her and your sister all the time Darien, what am I supposed to think? Tonya was your first love, and I do not care what you went through with her. You still have some feelings for her. You're always tired when you come home, and you have no time for me-" She's interrupted as Darien's cell phone rang.

"Hold on a minute Dutch," Darien speaks into the phone. "Tish let me take this call, see what the girls doing in there. I have to talk to Dutch for a few."

Tish got up, wiped her face, and fixed her clothes before walking into the kitchen. Darien watched her and resumed talking. Once she was out of the room, he knew he had a problem on his hands. He felt that Tish was not believing a word he says. What he's learned all these years they've been married is that she is very good at putting things together and can smell that shit a mile away. He does not know how she found out that Tonya was always hanging around his sister's house. One thing he had to do was find out who was talking.

"Hey, Dutch, is everything alright?" Darien changed his tone.

"Yeah man, how's things there, I know you handled that."

"Of course I did, shit's good here. You know I'm not gonna let nothing happen to my family."

"When you coming down to the club?"

"I'll be there in a few," said Darien. "I was just talking to Tish about some crazy mess, but I'll see you in a minute man."

"Yeah, alright, nothing that I can't handle. Everything will be good. Once we move out of here. I'll talk to you about that when I see you, alright man? Later."

Darien called Tish into the living room. As she walked in, she noticed him gathering things together, like his keys, his wallet, and his phone charger, and knew he was on his way out.

"Where are you going?" she asked.

“Look Tish, I got to get you away from here. I want you to start packing and I want you to start tonight, and as soon as we can we’re out of here, you hear me?”

“Are you going to look for a place now, Darien? I mean, really?” Tish sarcastically asked. “No, I have to meet up with Dutch. He got something for me. I’ll be right back, and don’t worry, everything’s going to be alright.” he said. while walking out the door.

Chapter 2

Darien nervously walked down to the club and looked behind to see if anyone was following. He quickly dashed inside and looked around until he spotted Dutch, sitting at the bar with three young ladies standing around him with their drinks lined up on the counter. He knew what the deal was. Dutch wasn't aware of Darien's presence until he felt hot air on his neck. Dutch turned around to see where it was coming from and saw Darien standing there, eyeing him like he lost his mind.

"What do you call yourself doing?" Darien questioned him while looking at the ladies up and down. It was a full house, and the music was pumping. Any other time Darien would've taken a seat and joined in the conversation. That night, though, all he had on his mind was money and getting his family away to a safer neighborhood. He stood there waiting for an answer, wondering how much Dutch had spent on the ladies. He was there for a long time and could've done a lot of damage.

"Oh, here my man go right here. Ladies, this is Darien, the man," Dutch introduces him, "and Darien, these are the most beautiful young ladies you could ever meet." Dutch drunkenly tries to point, "This is Carmen, and this is Sherry, and this cute little thing right here is Samantha. Say hello to my main man Darien." Darien reached for their hands, barely touching them and greeting each one.

"He's good-looking," said Sherry.

Dutch turned and looked directly at her, "Yeah, he may be good-looking, but don't try it 'cause he's taken *twice*." They all started laughing, but not Darien. He didn't think it was funny at all.

He looked at Dutch, "Come on man, I ain't got time for this right now. I need to talk to you, let's get up out of here."

"Excuse us ladies, me and the man got to take care of some business," Dutch says, struggling to get off the barstool. "I'll be right back." He smacked Samantha on the butt. "Keep my seat warm for me," he said, as he led Darien to the men's room.

"Just step into my office for a minute." Darien followed him, shaking his head.

"You know you cannot drink, Dutch. Why you got so much in front of you?"

"Shit, I'm gonna need somebody to cuddle up with, Darien." said Dutch. "How much did you spend there, start counting, it's a lot of money. The day I stopped there was 1500 and I wasn't even halfway through."

"What happened, man?"

"That damn ATM machine started malfunctioning. It kept telling me my account was empty but after I kept hitting that sucker a couple of times, it started coughing up $20 bills like crazy." He wasn't through with counting when someone entered the restroom. He put everything away and acted like he was using the bathroom. After few minutes it was just Dutch and Darien in the men's room, still counting.

"It's time to go, Dutch," Darien mumbles, not losing his count. "Time to go, I have to find an apartment quick. I'm getting Tish and the girls away from here. I don't know where, but anywhere will be better than where we're at now."

"I know where you can find a three-bedroom apartment in East Orange. Are you looking for a better neighborhood in Newark?"

"East Orange would be good. Do you know something?"

"Yeah, I'll write down the name and address and you can go check it out tonight." "This time of night?" Darien asked.

"These people keep the late hours anyway. Go check it out and call me in the morning."

"Will do," said Darien, leaving the men's room and waving at the ladies as he walked past. He was so happy to get back in his car, he hugged and kissed the steering wheel. Darien slowly drove up Central Avenue in Newark until he got to East Orange. *Okay, this looks much better* he thought to himself. *It looks like all homeowners live on this block. I hope Dutch is right about coming here. So late, if somebody rings my doorbell this time of night talking about some apartment I'll go off. I forgot to ask him if there was a dog on the premises* he thought as he walked up on the porch looking around.

"This is nice. I mean really nice, and it has a backyard for the girls. I love it already." Darien murmurs, before ringing the bell. A door opened, and a tall, dark-skinned man stood in front of him with a frown on his face, "May I help you?"

"Sir, I'm sorry for ringing your bell this time of night, but a friend of mine told me it would be okay, so I took a chance..."

“What’s your friend’s name?”

“Dutch. Dutch Wilson?” Darien said, hoping the man remembered the name.

“Oh, okay. I know who you’re talking about. Well, it’s a three bedroom, $1400 a month, utilities not included, ‘n a month and a half advance. Do you want to see it?”

“Yes, I do.” “Follow me.”

“Sir, it’s just what I was looking for,” Darien says as he looks around. *She’s gonna love it. Large living room, three huge windows (which I’m gonna have to cover with plastic soon to save money on the heat bill), dining room, and three bedrooms. I wouldn’t have any work to do in here like the other place. I know one thing, I better grab it now, while I got the money before someone comes and snatches this up.* “Excuse me, sir, how soon can I give you the rent and security?”

“You can give me the security now if you like. And pay the rent when you move in.”

“Is there an application to fill out?”

“Hmm, you know paperwork,” said Darien. “I didn’t say there was”

“Okay, I just thought...”

“No, once you mention Dutch I know you’re alright. I’ll give you a receipt and that would be good enough.”

“Thanks, man, thank you so much. I really appreciate this; how soon can I move in?”

“Well, I’ll tell you Darien the apartment is ready right now there’s nothing else to be done here. I can give you the keys now if you like.”

"That sounds like a plan to me, sir. I will see you in the morning."

Darien was on his way back to Newark as happy as could be thinking. This would make Tish feel better about what happened earlier. Now he just has to find out who's starting trouble by telling Tish what's going on at his sister's house. He thought about it the whole day, and how it could have turned out if he had made the wrong move. There was a minute when Bobby had the gun on him that he actually felt sorry for him. They knew each other's family. They grew up together and had dinner together. He tried to figure out where his grade school buddy went wrong in his life to bring harm to his own people, and for that, one day, he was going to get him back. But first, he must get his family to a safer place. Darien parked the car in front of the chicken restaurant and ran into the place to order before calling Tish.

He explained everything to her, except the money that came out of the ATM machine. He decided it was not the right time for that and he didn't want her to start worrying about him going to jail. As soon as the sun rose the next morning, Darien laid restlessly in bed, eyes wide open and thoughts racing. He mentally organized the whole day, making sure that everything would go well. He had enough money for the security and a few months' rent which he decided to give to Dutch. Just in case anything were to happen to him, Tish and the girls would be taken care of for a while.

Three hours later, he got up out of bed and walked down the hall to the bathroom. It's 8 am Saturday and everyone is still asleep. He quickly bathed and went to the kitchen to fix breakfast. The smell of the bacon frying and the biscuits in the oven got Tish and the girls up. Passing by the kitchen, rubbing their eyes on the way to the bathroom. The girls managed to let out a "good morning" as Tish entered the kitchen to watch Darien put the last touches on, what he called, his masterpiece breakfast.

"When will the truck be here?" Tish asked, and she watched Darien place the food on the table.

"One hour to be exact," He replied.

"That doesn't give us enough time."

"Enough time for what?" Darien asked.

"To help put the stuff on the truck, what do you think, you want us to help right?"

"If you want, just do what you have to do to get yourself ready. Dutch and I can get things started." Darien handled the business with the landlord. After bringing in the last of the boxes heavily filled with books Darien and Tish left Dutch with the girls to go back to the old apartment to clean up and return the keys. That was the only way they would be able to collect their security deposit.

While Darien handled the business with the landlord, Tish walked around the corner to their favorite chicken wing place to get a few pieces to go with their dinner. She waited outside the store for almost 30 minutes after she purchased, standing patiently, waiting with chicken and fries, periodically going in and out of the bag nibbling.

"What could be taking him so long?" she mumbled to herself. "This is not like Darien. I hope that landlord's not giving him any trouble. The rent was not paid on time every month, but we made damn sure it was paid before the month was out with late fees, of course. If that nasty old man gave him any trouble, I'm letting the cat out the bag and telling Darien about all those times he tried to get fresh with me. I should've told him a while ago."

She ate a few more fries and decided to walk back to the apartment, knowing that she was going to catch Darien running his mouth. But when Tish arrived, she saw the car still parked in the same place. They left it when they went into the building, and the landlord was at his usual sweeping in front of the house. "Excuse me, John, did Darien meet you yet?"

John stopped sweeping and started going through the trash as if he were looking for something, "Yeah, we met. We sure did and he left."

"Did he say where he was going?" Tish asked.

"No, as a matter of fact, he didn't. He left out in a hurry. When he first got here, he said you was around the corner. I thought maybe he would wait here for you, but he didn't."

"And I've been around there waiting all this time," she shook her head.

She watched him search through the trash and pull up a bright shiny men's bracelet. "He never showed up, that's why I walked around here. That's not like him at all, and why would he leave his car? Damn car was probably giving him trouble again. I'm going to the bus stop to wait there. **Please let** him know that I'm standing out there waiting for him. Either him or the bus, whichever comes first," she shook her head.

"Oh sure, I will," John nods. "And I wish you luck in your new place."

"Thank you, John, you take care of yourself, okay?" Tish walked off, turning her head back to see John watching her.

As he stood there, putting the silver chain bracelet on his arm, she waved goodbye. He slowly nodded at her, which gave her a creepy feeling. Tish thought about the crush he had on her since they'd been living there. John is a tall, dark, heavy man, about the age of 60 with a muscular build. Tish always felt uncomfortable around him and never trusted him. He had a crush on her and had been making passes at her since the first day they moved in 10 years ago. Tish and Darien had only been dating for three months before Darien asked to marry him and she was pregnant at the time, which John knew.

When they first moved in, she told him that she was pregnant while he stared at her breast. Tish told him it was none of his business and to keep his eyes where they belonged. There were a few more times Tish had to cuss John out after he started making comments about her body. It got worse when his wife passed away from cancer about a year after they moved in, she never said a word to Darien.

Tish is pretty brave when it comes to standing up for herself, so she would never let anyone take advantage of her. She tried to handle all and any disputes on her own before confronting Darien. She knew she had to be a strong person. She could handle John on her own. She also knew it would cause problems for them in the long run as they lived there, Darien would be watching John like a hawk. Anything that seemed out of pocket or disrespectful would have been the end of John, and apartments were so hard to come by. She knew she had to do all she could to keep that one.

Standing at the bus stop waiting for the 94-bus going to East Orange Tish thought about what could have happened to Darien, and why would he just leave his car like that? She thought to herself, *well he must be taking care of business. I'll catch up with him later. The new apartment is great. Hopefully, Darien will be at home more often instead of at his sister Regina's house. She called and everything, but I just don't trust her friend Tonya, she ain't fooling me a bit. She still wants Darien, and I know she hates the fact that he's married to me because he never asked her. If it was not for me getting my little fix every now and then that situation would have drove me crazy. All those nights I called Regina and as we were talking, I would hear Darien and Tonya laughing in the background. Just having a good time while I sit at home waiting for him, and he's trying to tell me nothing is going on and that they're just friends. I don't think so...*

Tish looked over her surroundings. There were a few people standing at the bus stop: a young, obese woman, standing with a cane, shifting her weight back and forth. A school-age teen rapping to the music blasting through his headphones. There was just one particular guy who caught her eye while looking back behind her. He looks to be in his early 40s. He stood with his back straight and tall. He was dressed neat and clean, cut and shaved. She admired the pink and white striped shirt he was wearing. She felt that a man who wears pink is not afraid to show his feminine side and not quick to anger. She noticed him constantly checking his watch and read into that as if he was running late for work, which had to be a night job.

He started pacing back and forth, checking the time on his watch. Tish surprised herself when she opened her mouth and blurted out, “Hey, it’s too hot for all that,” and waited nervously for a response. Sometimes, you just can’t call out to strangers. The man looked up and around to see where the voice was coming from.

“Excuse me, too hot for what?” he asked while looking her up and down.

“Too hot for all that pacing back and forth, it must be about 90° out here and you’re about to wear a hole in the cement” He let out a laugh. Tish felt good about that response calmed down a bit. She continued, “I’m sure she’ll understand if you’re a little late.”

“You’re right,” he said, nodding his head a few times. “I’m just a little nervous and it’s not a she who’s waiting, it’s a he.”

“O-oh, I’m sorry...I didn’t know, I mean I didn’t... Well, he’s a lucky guy.”

“It’s not what you think, ma’am,” he explained.

“It’s quite all right, you don’t have to explain.” she quickly said, putting both her hands up to let him know that he could stop explaining.

He let out another laugh and this time moved closer to her so he was not talking too loud, "It's my son, ma'am, he's having a recital at his school tonight and I promised him I'd be there on time."

"Okay, okay, I feel you on that. I have two girls."

"That's nice," he hummed, extending his hand out. "I am Khalif, and you are?"

"Tisha, but everybody calls me Tish."

"Nice to meet you, Tish."

"Same here. What, is it a music concert?"

"No, a dance recital. He's into modern dancing." As they begin to engage in everyday small talk, a car comes speeding around the corner. Slamming on the brakes, trying not to hit a woman, it crossed the street and immediately slammed on the gas before taking off, screeching up the street as another car followed, spraying bullets in the air aimlessly.

The first car crashed into a parked car, and three men jumped out and started running. The guys in the second car immediately followed after, abandoning their vehicle. The people on the street started running for cover, ducking behind cars and running into alleys as the shots continued.

Tish and Khalif took off, running in the same direction. The closest place was an alley with a wide, but short fence. Tish threw her pocketbook and bag over the fence. Khalif put both hands on Tish's waist to lift her up as she grabbed hold of the top of the fence and jumped over. Khalif caught up with her as she continued to run towards the back of the yard, still hearing the screams and cries of someone who she believed just got shot.

They looked at each other in shock.

"What do we do?" Tish asked while trying to catch her breath.

"I guess it's okay to wait back here for a while until everything calms down." Khalif looked around the yard for a place for them to sit and rest. He noticed a small bench that was placed against the house, directly under an open window. He motioned for Tish to join him on the bench, leaning over and whispering in her ear, "Do not talk loud." He pointed at the window.

"I hope I don't see no one running out of this back door, shooting at us thinking we were trying to rob the place" he laughed.

A few moments passed when Khalif decided to walk towards the front to see if the coast was clear. He looked over the gate then up and down the street and saw nothing. He assumed the bus had already passed by because there was no one standing out there. He waited for Tish to follow him, "Come on, it's okay we can leave them."

She followed him, but just as they both started climbing over the gate, they heard the gunshots again and had to retreat to the backyard.

"It started up again," Tish said in disbelief.

"I don't know how long we're going to have to be back here, but I do know that it's the safest place right now."

"Well, we better get comfortable if we have to wait it out," said Tish.

"This is unbelievable, no matter how hard I try, I just cannot seem to get to this recital. I'm really late and my son is going to be disappointed thinking I'm not going to show up at all. All this chasing and gunfire, people running around screaming their heads off, this world is going crazy."

Tish grabbed the bag that she placed on the edge of the bench while listening to Khalif talk. She reached into the bag and pulled out a red and white box and opened it, "Would you like a piece of chicken while we wait?"

They both tried hard to contain the laughter as he reached into the box for a wing, "I'd know where you're coming from. It is crazy Khalif," she said, pulling the meat away from the bone with her teeth. "I just moved from around here to a much better place and I was on my way back there."

"Before all this mess started, why were you back on this side of town?" Khalif asked. "Well, my husband and I came to pick up our security deposit and clean the apartment up a little so we would get our deposit back, but I had no clue where he had disappeared to. Now I have to catch the bus back home to find out what happened to him."

"He's not answering his cell?" Khalif asked.

"No answer. Can you believe the car was still parked in front of the old apartment?" Khalif stop chewing, swallowed his food, and looked at Tish with concern, "That doesn't sound good at all."

"You are right Khalif, and I am worried. Do you live around here?" she asked him.

"No, I do not. I wanted to see if my son's mother was going to the recital. I had to loan her my car a few days ago until she got hers out of the shop, so I got over here from across town only to find no car parked in front of her house and no answer on her cell." They both had to let out a big laugh and quickly look back at the open window.

"Somebody's coming out of the door for sure. Now we better get from back here." They went from loud laughter to giggling and covering their mouth. "So, tell me about your son's mother," Tish asked.

"There's not much to tell really. She moved back here from Maryland so that I can help her out more with raising him. She left her wife in Maryland to finish up some last-minute business."

"Oh, okay, I see. How long have you two been divorced? One year, to be exact. How do you feel about the situation, then being married-" Tish stopped herself. "Oh, I'm sorry, I don't mean to be all in your business, you don't have to answer that."

"No, it's okay. Hey, she's happy and if she's happy, my son is happy." "Oh okay," Tish nodded her head.

"How old are your girls?" Khalif asked Tish.

"Ten and five. Very good girls, love them to death."

"I'm quite sure they feel the same for you. I hope everything's okay with your husband."

"Thank you so much Khalif. I'm praying everything is okay with him. I'm going to try to give him another call. I can't believe he hasn't called me yet." She shook her head while putting away what was left of the chicken and fries.

They heard a phone ringing from the open window. They just sat there, listening for a voice to answer, but it never happened. It just kept ringing while they were getting off the bench to make their way to the front of the house.

"We better get to the bus stop, it should be another one coming soon," said Tish.

The bus arrived on time and was letting on passengers as they made their way over the fence. They made a dash for it and jumped on the bus in time to see an ambulance drive off from an area that had yellow police tape. They watched as the bus made its way around the traffic of police cars and people looking at each other, shaking their heads in disbelief. They both took a seat on the opposite side of the aisle.

Tish leaned over and whispered to Khalif, "This has been a crazy day for me. Never thought I would be hanging out in someone's backyard, a stranger's yard at that with a stranger." They both laughed out loud.

"You're right about that, the same here," said Khalif. They talked and laughed for a while before Khalif stood up.

"This is my stop here." He said, reaching out his hand to shake hers. "Well Tish, it was nice meeting you, regardless of the circumstances, I'm glad I did meet you."

"Same here, Khalif I haven't been last like this in a long time. I hope we meet again on a more pleasant occasion."

"Hopefully, you enjoy the rest of your evening, what's left of it," Khalif said as he walked towards the front of the bus. He looked back at her as he stepped down to exit, "and good luck on your new place."

"Thank you so much," she replied and waved goodbye.

Chapter 3

Tish got off at the next stop, wondering what could have happened to Darien as she quickly walked down her block. She searched her pocketbook to make sure she had the keys. She thought she had given them to Darien as she was near the new home. She looked up at the window and saw no one. *Dutch and the girls have been waiting a long time for us to get back. I hope Dutch fixed them some dinner. I hate it when the girls go looking for snacks, tearing the kitchen up for me to clean it up.*

She walked up the stairs of the porch, and as soon as she put the keys in the door and turned it, the door swung open. Tish stood there, with her mouth wide open, waiting for Dutch to speak first.

"What is it? What's going on Dutch?" she asked as she stood in the doorway, staring at him.

"Is Darien-"

"He got into some trouble," the look on Dutch's face told her it was a very bad trouble. She stood there, trying to prepare herself for the worst.

Her heart started beating fast, and her breathing became out of control, "Tell me Dutch, tell me what happened to Darien. Is he hurt? Where is he?" she screamed.

"He's not hurt, Tish." She felt instant relief. "He got locked up and I think it's not going to be any bail. I'm hoping he's not going to be gone for a long time, but it doesn't look good Tish." Tish dropped to the floor of the hallway, shaking her head in disbelief. Dutch sat next to her and put his arm around her.

"What could he have possibly done to get himself locked up? He never breaks the law. Darien doesn't do anything but work. He don't mess with drugs. He's not a troublemaker,

he always respected authority. Dutch, tell me what could have got him locked up!" she screamed.

"Tish, it's crazy, it's just something that happened. Darien knew he was doing something wrong, but he had to do what he had to do so his family could be in a better place. It was just one of those situations, we talked about it for a while, him and I, and we knew that one day it was going to catch up with him, but we thought he had way more time than this."

"Is it all of that money he's been having lately? Is that what it is?" Tish asked.

"Yeah, it did have something to do with that." Dutch nodded.

"Did he rob somebody?" she yells.

"No, no, no, Darien would never do that. You know that, SHHHH!!!" He put his finger to her mouth. "They might hear you."

"Come on Dutch, tell me."

"Okay, there was a lot of money, and it was coming out of the ATM machine a few days ago before you guys moved here. Darien hit the machine a couple of times trying to get the money out for those guys that had you and the girls held up in the house." Tish started crying. "The first thing he wanted to do, Tish, is to get you and the girls away from those thugs. He thought they were going to try to come back when he was not at home."

"He knew the camera was in that bank, but he just didn't know how long it would take before they caught up with him."

Between the lump in her throat and crying, she was barely able to talk, "I can't believe this is happening. Not to us. It's just too much for me to handle-" Dutch reached into his pocket and pulled out his wallet. He opened it and started counting money, she just looked at him and told him to put it back and to put his wallet away.

"Look Tish, this is what he wanted me to do and I promised him I would do it. I promised him that I would take care of you and the girls while he was away Tish."

"If I need anything, I will let you know. I don't want that money in my hands right now."

"Tish, I'm sorry this had to happen to you guys and I'll-" She stood up and picked up her pocketbook and started up the stairs.

"You should've stopped him. You should've made him put that money on the floor and leave out of there and that's what the cameras would have shown. I can't believe you Dutch, you could've stopped him."

"Tish, you know yourself can't nobody stop Darien from doing something he wants to do. Not me, you, or nobody else.

He was upset and hurt. He was bleeding and he worried about you and the girls. He didn't care about spending time in jail as long as you and the girls was safe."

"What about Tonya? Did she get anything? Did he give her any money?"

Dutch stood, motionless, and shocked to hear those words coming from Tish's mouth. He didn't know what to say. He didn't know exactly how to answer it. He definitely didn't know how much Darien told her about Tonya, he was afraid he was going to say too much or not enough.

"Dutch, don't stand there and act like you don't know what I'm talking about."

"I don't know Tish, and I don't want to discuss this with you. Talk to Darien about that mess when you go to visit him."

"I cannot talk to Darien about shit at this moment now can I Dutch??" Tish was at the top of the stairs now, about to close the door on Dutch.

"Don't do this to me, Tish. I know things were not right with us when we first met, but I've been in you and Darien's life too long for us to be going through this. Call me later so you can let me know if you need anything. I love you girl, and I'm sorry again."

Tish didn't open her mouth. She just sighed as she closed the door, not knowing if he was still standing there or not. She walked to her bedroom, sat on the edge of the bed and cried.

Chapter 4

Tish spent the last two months decorating the apartment, caring for the girls, helping them with their schoolwork, and writing Darien (although Darien never wanted her to work outside the house and talked her out of many job openings). She felt that now was a good time to start looking for work, so she decided to start searching for real estate schools to get a license to sell homes. That was something she was always interested in doing before she started her family. Darien always felt that caring for him and the girls was enough work and anything else would take her away from what she needed to do for them. He told her that there would have to be some sacrifice, and he didn't want it to be the girls.

Darien's been working for the Housing Authority for 15 years. It was his first job when he graduated from high school. Work, home, and his sister's house or the occasional night out on the town for a movie or dancing was all she would see of Darien. He was more committed to the girls, entertaining them when he was at home. Darien was content with his life, but Tish wanted more. She always felt it was something missing in her life and she just couldn't put a finger on it. She had an emptiness inside, a yearning and loneliness that nagged her constantly. She didn't want Darien to know that she was using again, but she felt she had to do something, or she would not have been able to stay with Darien too much longer. He spent so much time away from home, she felt she wouldn't miss him anyway. Tish couldn't bring herself to take the girls away from Darien.

They are his whole life. For now, she just satisfied herself with a little cocaine and her snacks, sodas, and chips whenever Darien went to sleep. It took three months for Tish to receive her license in real estate and she graduated at the top of her class. She immediately started her job search at various real estate offices, leaving a trail of resumes. She kept Darien informed of her progress, and although he was not happy about her decision to go back to work, he congratulated her on her accomplishment. Now that he's going to be incarcerated for a while, he figured it would be something to keep her busy besides caring for the girls.

While Tish was doing the breakfast dishes, her cell phone rang. She dried her hands and picked it up. She saw that it was Darien. He asked how everyone was doing and talked about some books he was reading. They didn't stay on the line long, he told her he'd give her a call in a few days. That's how it was for a few months, they would never talk long when they were on the phone and the calls were spaced days apart. One thing she was grateful for was Darien moving them to a better neighborhood, which is the best thing he could have ever done for his family.

A year has gone by already. Tish cannot believe how fast time has flown by. It was the last day of school and she planned to take the girls to Dorney Park, she told Dutch to be at the house by 1 o'clock. The girls had a half day and should be home by 12. Dutch was on time but the girls hadn't come home yet and Tish started to worry.

It's now 12:40pm and that was long enough for Tish. Shakima and Rahanna are always on time.

"I don't know what could have happened. Today of all days, come on Dutch. We have to go out and look for them."

"We both can't go," said Dutch. "Suppose they show up while we're gone."

"You're right Dutch, I'm not thinking straight," Tish shook her head with a nervous tremble in her voice.

Dutch hugged her, and kissed her on the forehead, "I'll be right back with the girls, do not worry. They probably stopped off to talk to some friends. It would be a couple of months before they see their friends again, I know that much," said Dutch as he exited the front door.

Dutch walked up Central Avenue, searching every crowd and eyeing every child he passed. He checked inside the bodegas, small grocery stores, and candy shops. When Dutch reached the school grounds, he saw nothing and no one. There was not a child in sight. Dutch started racing around the school, checking locked doors. All he heard was echoes from everywhere. He ran around to the front of the building and noticed a tall man dressed in janitor work clothes and asked if anyone was left in the office, and that he was looking for two girls.

The janitor assured him that there was no one left in the building. He also informed him that there were a few young girls on the corner of the school playing and laughing and that they turned the corner about 20 minutes ago. Dutch thanked the man and took off in that direction, hoping he could catch up with the girls. His heart started racing and sweat poured down his face as he hurled down the street. All he could think of was the look on Tish's face if he walked into the house without the girls, there was no way he could go back there without them.

He continued to search up and down the street, turning his head towards any alleys and driveways he passed on the path the girls should have taken home. He frantically turned the corner when he noticed a man. The back of the man looked familiar.

He called out his name, "Darien, Darien, that you?" Darien and the girls all turned around to see who it was screaming out his name.

"Oh no, this is unbelievable. Are you really standing there or am I dreaming?" He said with his mouth wide open. "When did you get out Darien?" Dutch asked while running up to him. Darien searched him over with his eyes, still not believing in what he was seeing. They grabbed and hugged each other.

"I got out about an hour ago man, I came straight here since I had time before girls got out of school."

"Well damn, you could've called someone. Me and Tish was worrying like crazy about the girls. We're supposed to be on our way to Dorney Park."

"Yeah, the girls were just telling me about that. Well, you've got one more on board," Darien said while laughing. He gave the girls a hug, "Come on little ladies, let's go surprise your mama."

They headed towards home. Dutch looked Darien up and down again as they walked, "Man, you can do some crazy shit."

"Yeah, you're right about that, my friend," said Darien. He stopped in front of a man sitting on a bench at the gas station and started picking out some flowers for Tish. He paid the man and started back to the house.

Dutch noticed Darien looking down at the flowers. He knew what he was thinking, "She's doing good, Darien. Tish knows how to hold it down. That's a strong woman you got there. I think you're the luckiest man in the world."

"Did she talk about me much?"

"Hey, I'm not gonna lie to you. She barely mentioned your name but you know, I can tell you were heavy on her mind.

She was very upset when I told her what happened, she cussed me out."

Darien started laughing but suddenly stopped when he thought about the possibility of her using again. Dutch caught that look and immediately jumped up, "She's clean man. Going on interviews, to libraries, and visiting the girls' school. I'm telling you she doing her thing." When they arrived at the house Darien asked Dutch to stay downstairs with the girls for a few minutes. He walked up the stairs and stood there for a moment before knocking at the door.

Chapter 5

Tish took a small bottle from the kitchen cabinet, opened it, and shook two pills out into the palm of her hand. Shaking, she reached for a glass and filled it halfway with water. She looked down at the two pills, and then put them both in her mouth, drank the water, hoping the little white pills would take away what she felt was the worst headache ever, before placing the bottle in the sink.

She glanced out the window wondering what was taking Dutch so long, if everything was okay, they should've been back by now. Without realizing it, her fingers loosened from the grip they had on the glass. It hit the sink.

The noise of the shattering glass took her out of the trance. She was suddenly locked in. She fixed her eyes on the man standing in the window of a building across the yard, she had seen him once before. She recognized him from somewhere, his face, his hair, the way he nodded his head as he spoke on the phone. Her memory took her back to the day she was at the bus stop, waiting at the chicken place for Darien for hours. She could not believe what she was seeing. *No, this is not him,* she said to herself in her mind, *he just wasn't real.* She remembered his name. She watched him for a while as he moved around his apartment, room to room, window to window.

She had to rush from the window to answer the door.

"You girls are going to be the death of me," she yelled while swinging the door open, thinking she was going to see her two young ladies standing there with long faces thinking they were in trouble since Dutch had to come looking for them, but instead she saw Darien standing in front of the door. She immediately retreated into shock mode.

First with Khalif, and now Darien, her mouth dropped open as her arms fell to her side. It's been two years and Tish was at a loss for words, and all she could do was bury herself in Darien's embrace. When Tish gained enough strength, she put her arms around Darien again, it was nothing like she imagined. Tish had a mental picture in her head. *I'm standing outside the prison gates, waiting for Darien to walk through.* She played it over and over in her head for two years.

"It's been a long time, baby," were the first words that came out of Darien's mouth.

"Oh, Darien, the girls went-" He stopped her.

"The girls are fine, they're downstairs with Dutch. I just wanted a few minutes alone with you. That's if you don't mind, of course."

"I don't mind," she said, smiling. Darien kissed her several times on the cheek before he entered the apartment. She followed him as he walked through the hall to put his duffel bag and briefcase on the floor of the bedroom.

"So, you work sweetie?"

"I took the opportunity to make our lives a little better, and I knew it was a risk, but I had to do it anyways. Is that all you want to hear? Because that's all I have to tell you," Tish just looked him in the eyes. "I'm not even thinking about myself, Darien. You took time away from your girls, don't you think they needed you?"

"Look, I'm sorry Tish, if I made things hard for you and the girls in any way, but I'm home now. I want to make it up to you and them," he picked her up. "Am I forgiven?" he asked, looking her in the eyes. She tried hard not to look at him. She was trying to stay in a serious mood.

"Am I forgiven?" he asked again, and she started laughing.

"Yes, yes, yes, you are. Okay now put me down so we can go spend some time with the family." The weather cooled down a little with a nice light breeze as the sun started to descend. The park was still crowded with long lines at the rides. Darien and Tish watched the girls ride for a while as they talked and ate pizza, funnel cake, and cotton candy before Darien decided to join the girls on some of the rides. Tish just stood there and laughed as they spun around on the Cyclones. A few hours later, after walking around and taking pictures, Tish asked Darien to ride the merry-go-round with her.

"Anything for my queen," he said as he helped her up on the wooden horse. "Hold on tight now, it's gonna be a rough ride," he teased.

"Okay, so you wanna be like that? When we finish with this, I challenge you to the Ferris wheel" she laughed. Tish knew Darien did not like heights, especially when he wasn't in control and couldn't get down when he wanted to.

"Crazy lady, you won't get me on that thing," she tried not to laugh, but it slipped out.

"Why Darien? Is it too rough for you?" she yelled.

"Oh okay, it's on. You think I'm scared, don't you?"

"I know you are," she said.

"Miss Kindle, you do not know me very well," he told her with raised eyebrows.

The girls watched as their parents ascended into the air, higher and higher, and slowly back down again as they waited with excitement. Darien had his eyes closed, hoping Tish wouldn't notice, "I can't remember the last time we were on this very Ferris wheel."

"Before the girls came along. You had a fit, trying to yell down for the guy to let you down so you could get off."

"That's because there was something wrong with this thing. It wouldn't stop shaking, remember?" Tish burst into laughter.

"Your eyes are closed, Darien."

"No, they're not," he lied.

"You're lying, Darien. Your eyes are closed," she laughed again.

"It's been a long time since I've been up this high. Maybe I am a little nervous" Tish thought about the last time they were on this ride. They were so much in love and couldn't keep their hands off each other. Darien couldn't stand when another man looked at her.

Things are different now, Tish is no longer overwhelmed with emotions, with the deep, heartfelt passion that she felt for Darien back then. Things just changed too much between them. She watched him as they rode down and back up again. He looked to be in deep thought, like his mind was somewhere else. She truly believed that Tonya was on his mind. She wanted to ask him, but he beat her to it, "What's on your mind, Tish?"

He placed his arms around her neck, bringing her closer to him.

"I'm just sorry I didn't get a chance to visit you like I should have," she put her head down.

"I knew you had a lot on your plate. The letters were good enough."

"Really?" she asks, not believing him.

"Sure sweetie, they got me through the rough days. Every time I had to go through some mess, I would pick up one of your letters and start reading, then all of a sudden, a smile would come to my face. I would go through all the pictures and then I would feel better," he kissed her on the cheek.

For the rest of the ride, they were silent, just observing the view.

Chapter 6

Tish joined Darien in the bedroom and watched as he threw some of his clothes into the wardrobe. He held up a pair of faded jeans, "These are going to the trash." He held up another pair, "And so are these." He threw a few of his shirts into a pile.

"Darien, those clothes are still good, why are you throwing them away?"

"I put on weight baby, and I might not drop these pounds for a long time because I'm about to eat some good home cooking," he laughed. Darien grabbed the clothes and threw them in a large plastic garbage bag, "I'll be back, sweetie. I'm gonna take this bag down to the garbage room."

He tied the bag and walked towards the front door, stopping to peek at the girls and say good night.

"Are you sure you're coming back?" Tish said in a joking manner. "The last time I waited for you was the longest wait ever."

"You've been very humorous today, dear, but whatever makes you happy. You just be ready for me to take care of my husbandly duties when I get back."

She smiled and watched him as he walked out the door before slowly walking to the kitchen, stopping at the large mirror to look at herself up and down. She noticed a little weight gain and made a mental note to start an exercise program. *All I have to do is stop buying potato chips and soda at the store. I'll be alright,* she thought to herself. Tish turned on the kitchen light and walked over to the sink.

She then noticed a light come on through Khalif's window while she was reaching for a glass. She watched as he moved around from room to room, wondering if anyone was there with him.

Why wouldn't there be? she thought to herself. *Khalif is a very handsome man, and he definitely knows how to hold a conversation. The last time we talked left a lasting impression on me. He's not a mama's boy, but I can tell by the way he talks that he loves and respects his mother to the fullest, and that's an important quality in a man. I like that.*

He shouldn't have any problem with having a woman in his life. He's gonna make some woman very happy one day, and that's if he's not doing it right now. Well, in any event, I wish him all the happiness, he deserves it. Let me get out this window and get my mind off this man, shame on me, she scolded herself. But just as she was about to draw the curtains their eyes met.

At first, Khalif wasn't sure of who he was looking at and whether she was really looking at him. It took him a minute to focus when he finally realized it was Tish. He waved with a surprised expression on his face, and she waved back. He pointed to the building and then at her twice, asking if she lived there. Tish nodded yes, and he nodded back with a smile.

"Tish?" Darien called from the bedroom. "Coming, just give me a second."

"What are you doing in there?" He asked.

"Oh, nothing Darien, I just finished a glass of water. Do you want anything before I come in there?"

No, I'm good." Tish waved goodbye to Khalif and got out the window nervously before he got a chance to wave back.

She tried to figure out why she was so excited suddenly, it was not the same excitement she had when she saw Darien at the door earlier, nor was it the same excitement that she had at the amusement park. This feeling was totally different, and it felt good. She walked into the bedroom, unaware of the smile on her face, thinking about the meal her and Khalif shared in the stranger's backyard. For some strange reason, the chicken she had that night was the best she ever had. Or was it because of the person she was sharing it with?

"I hope that smile on your face is because you're happy to see me lying in our bed again," Darien smiled, reaching his arms out to Tish.

"I'm glad you're home Darien, you were missed," was all she could say. She was in bed now, pulling the cover over her shoulders, moving closer to Darien. It was awkward at first, being that she felt alone for almost 2 years.

"Do you want me to turn the air off, Tish?" "No," she replied. "Why would you do that?"

"Because you're under the cover like you're cold," he shrugged, putting his arm on her shoulder.

"I'm okay, Darien. The water I just drank was cold, that's all."

"The girls had a great time today. They were so happy to see you back home. I told them everything Darien, I didn't want-." She paused. "I didn't want to, but you were gone for so long and

I didn't want them to find out what happened from anyone else but me, they were asking so many questions."

Tish waited for a moment, wanting Darien to respond. When he didn't say a word she continued, "They were very quiet at first, and got a little depressed until it started to sink in. I think they were more worried about me. You coming home was just in time, perfect with all of us going to Dorney Park. They enjoyed it so much."

Tish looked around the room. White painted walls, the solid burgundy, floral print curtains that hung from the bedroom window was the focus point of the room. Flowers with earth tone-colored petals and green leaves set the mood of tranquility. Darien always complimented her on her decorating, always telling her that she should go into business being an interior designer, but she really wasn't interested in doing it as a career. She just enjoyed decorating her home for her family.

Tish took a deep breath. She laid there, wondering why Darien hadn't moved an inch. She called his name, and when he didn't respond, she looked up and saw that he was fast asleep and probably hadn't heard a word she said. Tish gave him a light kiss on the cheek and closed her eyes; she was too excited to go to sleep.

Her thoughts traveled all the way back home to Mississippi. She was back in her mother's house with her mother and sister, who she hadn't seen in a long time. Tish is the oldest of the two and very close with her sister Patricia. She carries a lot of guilt for leaving her little sister behind with an occasional phone call or letter every now and then. That's all communication they've had between them for more than 15 years now, no more hand holding while walking down to the corner store and to their friend's house. No more hugs or loud outbursts of laughter, things have really changed between them.

Baby sis should understand why I had to leave. That day when mama found that joint in my pants pocket, she acted like she saw a needle going in my arm. She had no business searching through my pockets anyway, things would have been a lot worse if I had stayed home. All I needed was a little room to grow, being sheltered with just homework and housework all the time was bugging me out. Whenever I got home a little late from track practice she'd get on the phone and call the whole neighborhood checking up on me and checking out my story once I told her where I was (which was beyond embarrassing). I needed mama to trust me and let me make decisions for myself, and if it was the wrong decision, I had no one to blame but myself.

Tish finally fell asleep with her back turned towards Darien knowing deep down inside, she really didn't want the same thing he wanted.

7 AM the next morning Tish and Darien awakened to the sound of pounding at the door. Darien jumped out of bed and hurried to put his pajamas and slippers on. As he stumbled half asleep to the door, he could hear Dutch's voice yelling from the other side.

"Open up sleepy head. It's time to get up, we have places to go and people to see!"

Darien swung the door open, "You are about the most ghetto man I have ever met."

Dutch pushed his way through the door, "Look man, I told everybody at the job know that you are back home they want you to come in today."

"What?!! You're crazy, they wanna see me today?" Darien shook his head while walking into the living room for his cigarettes, leaving Dutch at the front door.

"Come on Darien," Dutch followed him into the living room. "I already told the guys that you would show up because you missed seeing them. All you've got to do is come in now."

He followed Darien over to the living room sofa before continuing, "You've still got some stash left but not enough to be sitting on your ass at home. When there's money to be made-"

"Man, give me my shit and wait here until I get dressed." Dutch made himself comfortable on the brown leather sofa, with his feet propped on the matching ottoman and the remote in his hand. He scanned for the morning news as he looked around the well decorated living room. He thought about how lucky Darien was to have a wife like Tish. He recognized her talent and was quite impressed with her interest in African art. Elephant statues, shiny beige acrylic with brown details with gold accents and eyes sat on each end of the coffee table, as well as pictures of African tribes, dancing and playing drums on dark green grass under the blue sky.

"You look very comfortable there, I almost hated to walk in and disturb you," Tish says as she hands him a cup of hot steamy coffee. "I see you're ready to go to work with your fresh clean uniform on. Darien can't fit his, he's gaining too much weight, he threw away some of his clothes last night."

Dutch sat straight up to receive his coffee, watching Tish but not really paying attention to what she was doing.

"How many sugars?" she asks, pointing to a few sugar packs in a dish.

"I guess you forgot, I don't put sugar, milk, or cream in my coffee."

"I sure did Dutch, sorry about that."

"It's okay, I forgive you this time but the next time though," he laughed out loud.

"Do not play with me. It's too early in the morning for that"

"I know that's right, and it's Saturday too. I know you're not trying to play, sleepyhead."

"You don't think it's too soon for Darien to be going back to work, do you?"

"No, not really. You know Darien hates sitting around the house, all he does is look around for things to do. His mind starts wandering like crazy"

Tish nodded, "Yeah, I guess you're right. He might start thinking about going back to the ATM machine."

"Hell yeah, let him go to work." They both laughed. Darien entered the living room, joining in with the laughter.

"Y'all talking about me, right?" Neither one answered, they couldn't stop laughing.

"Come on, Tish. Let's go."

"You silly people play too much," said Darien while walking toward the door, he thought about back in the day when they first met. He had to play referee when they would go word for word with each other in a rage.

He couldn't stand the fact that Tish was not getting along with Dutch. He didn't need his woman always arguing with his best friend. If Tish was right, Darien had to go against Dutch and vice versa. Both would get mad as hell when he told them to leave him out of it.

Tish thought Dutch had him out there cheating on her with all his female friends, and he sure kept a lot of them around him too. Darien never was a drinker. He could sit at a bar all night with one drink, but when he got home, Tish would blame Dutch for having him smelling like a liquor barrel. We all double dated when they first met Tish and Dutch would fuss over which movie theater to go to, which restaurant was better, whose car to take.

It would get so bad he could see in Dutch's eyes that he wanted to get at her, and she knew that. She would tell him to go ahead and try it. So yeah, Darien's glad all of that changed.

"I'm leaving the car here for Tish," he said looking at Dutch. "She might have to go out to get something today."

"That's cool, I'll tell you right now my car is a mess. Mr. Neat Freak," Dutch let out a laugh.

"Hey, well what can I say? Some people never change." Tish walked them to the door and watched as they headed for the stairs. She just stood there, leaning against the wooden door frame, with the bright sunlight beaming down on her from the window. Darien backtracked a few steps and looked at her.

"Did you forget something?" she asked.

"No, I didn't. I just want to let you know that I'm going to stop by my sister's house after work. I want to see how she's doing and play with the kids for a while. I'll call you when I get there."

He continued down the stairs without even waiting for a response. Tish closed the door, with so many thoughts starting to flood her mind. She felt an inkling of fear as she went straight to the kitchen to start breakfast for the girls. Just the thought of Darien walking into his sister's house and maybe right into Tonya's arms made her heart race.

There is more than what he's telling me. I cannot stand to be in a relationship where there's doubt, I'll need to be able to trust Darien. I need to be able to stand on solid ground. I can see a future with Darien, even though I don't love him the way I used to. He's the father of my girls, and I know I can try to make this work, I do want us to grow old together. There's so much that has yet to be done, events to attend: the girls' college, wedding plans, participating in the birth of our grandchildren. Darien needs to be with me through all of this, we can't break our family up. There is no room for Tonya in all of this and I don't want her involved. Darien can't just get up and leave to start another family like the drop of a hat. It's not that easy for me, I put my all into this relationship.

"Come on girls, time to get up, we got Saturday things to do! Laundry, shopping, cleaning, let's go!" Tish yelled as she stood in front of the girls' bedroom door. She looked at the large, red and white 'do not disturb' sign posted on the door, as well as a picture of the two both hanging on a nail at the top showing them lying in their twin beds asleep.

The picture was taken by Darien three years ago after a long day of roller-skating in the park. He took the picture near their bedroom clock to show the girls how fast they went to sleep. Tish thought that was really cute.

They swore to him that they were not tired. Tish and Darien laughed at the picture for weeks.

The girls were now in the kitchen having breakfast while watching their favorite Saturday morning program. Tish was in the living room debating whether she should pick up the phone and dial her sister-in-law, Regina. She hated the fact that she just happened to be calling her back after two years on the same day as Darien was showing up. She feels bad for not trying to reach out to her, to tell her why her brother was locked up. They're two years apart but look so much like twins and love each other to death. Regina showed some jealousy when Tish came into the picture. Darien had to assure her that no one would ever interfere with their sister and brother relationship, and that he just could not spend the time that he used to with her anymore because of his family.

Regina had to accept that, but she also told Tish that Darien was the glue that held their sister-in-law relationship together, and by Tish not calling her while Darien was incarcerated only proved that what she said was true. Tish picked the phone up and started dialing before hesitating for a moment.

Maybe Darien wants to surprise her, I don't want to mess it up for him, she thought to herself while biting off what little was left of her nails. The air conditioner in the living room was off and the hot sun was pouring in on her, making her sweat profusely. She continued dialing the number

"Hello?" a soft voice answered. "Hello Regina," Tish responded.

"No, this isn't Regina, may I take a message? She can't come to the phone at the moment." There was only silence when Tish realizes who she was talking to. She hated the fact that Tonya answered the phone and wanted desperately to hang it up. "Hello, may I ask who's calling? I am Tonya, a friend of Regina's."

"This is Tish, just tell them to give me a call. I see you are there so early in the morning?"

"I live here now, Tish."

"Oh, oh I see, how long have you been there?"

"Just a few months, it was a bit weird at first, but it seems to be working out pretty good now, so l decided to stay."

"I see," said Tish. "Anyways, just tell her I called, and I'll give her a call back later."

"Sure, I will," said Tonya. "Take care of yourself, Tish"

"You do the same, Tonya" Tish quickly hung up the phone before slowly easing up off the sofa in deep thought, trying to take in the conversation. She tried to picture what it was going to be like for Darien to be over there as much as he was before he was incarcerated.

She walked into the kitchen and saw that the girls hadn't finished their breakfast yet and started moving around the kitchen quickly cleaning up some of the mess they had made.

"Come on girls, we've gotta go to the library first before we do the laundry. It's gonna be a long day and there's too much to do for y'all to be still sitting there picking with the food. Now come on, let's go!" she yelled.

"Okay Mom, you do not have to get all bent out of shape. We just have to throw on our clothes real quick and we will be ready just like that."

"Oh, really? Just like that? We'll see."

"Why are you acting like that? What's wrong Mom? You just seem to be on edge this morning, is Dad ok?"

"He sure is, sweetie, now come on, let's get out of here and start our day."

Shakima reached her arms out to give Tish a hug, who slowly walked over to her, struggling to let out a smile. What she felt at that moment was pure love radiating through her body. She realized how much her daughter loved and appreciated her. She did not want her to see her hurt or upset. Shakima is 11, soon to be 12, yet she understands a great deal about family matters in relationships. Tish also realized at that moment that Shakima would soon be coming to her with a woman to woman talk and she is more than ready considering she still remembers the talk she had with her mother at 12.

Chapter 7

Tish walked in and out of the aisles in the library. She was not looking for any particular book, just something to read on the subject of real estate, something to add to the thousands of books she already had stacked up in the bedroom corner at home. The library was just about empty when they first arrived, though after two hours the place started filling up which meant that Tish had to search around for the girls. She was ready to go, and was not surprised when she didn't see either one of them at the location, they said they would be. Tish decided to just go outside to wait in front of the building, she needed a little air.

Once outside Tish took a deep breath in before slowly releasing the warm afternoon air from her lungs. She looked around at her surroundings, watching a car stop at the light on the corner. A man swept the grounds in front of the pharmacy across the street. He waved at her as if he knew her, she stood there for a while thinking about her conversation with Tonya this morning.

I know Tonya is going to tell Darien that I called she thrives off starting trouble, especially between me and Darien out of all his girlfriends or his so-called associates. She's the only one who's still in his life and seems to be having trouble letting him go. I still believe she's trying to take him away from me. I just cannot put my finger on it, but one day somebody is going to slip up and when that day comes......

Tish stepped aside, out of the way of the door as three middle school aged kids raced up the path. With a glimpse out the corners of her eyes she saw Shakima catching the door just before it closed, with Rahanna following behind her. Both had about four books apiece and were trying hard to handle them. Tish took one from the older girl and two from the youngest and hurried to the car.

Tish stopped at the grocery store before heading home. She filled the trunk with the bags, locked the car up, and walked over to the pizzeria for a few slices and soda. The girls wanted to eat there but Tish convinced them that it wouldn't be a good idea because they were already behind schedule and needed to start the laundry before sitting down to eat.

"Daddy might have some plans for us this evening. I still have to cook dinner, so we have to get everything done while leaving some time to freshen up," she explained.

"Oh, what about the movies? We haven't been in a while," Shakima requested.

"Sounds good to me. We'll see how daddy feels when he gets home," Tish responded while getting into the car and buckling up.

Darien was too exhausted to do anything when he returned home from work later that afternoon, he told Tish and the girls to give him a rain check on family night.

"Our work was really backed up at the housing complex." The girls understood, they stayed in their bedroom playing video games and watching television. Tish and Darien sat at the kitchen table eating, sitting across from each other, forking through their food and listening to the girls giggling from their bedroom. Tish was wondering if Darien knew that she called Regina today. She wanted to know how his visit went with his sister after two years, she wanted to know how it went seeing Tonya after two years. Despite her curiosity, Tish was determined not to bring it up first.

They were halfway through their meal when Darien asked for something to drink. This made Tish raise a brow, he never drinks while eating so the drinks would stay cold. They just kept it in the refrigerator until dinner was finished. Tish got up and walked over to the fridge and grabbed a bottle of carrot juice then placed it on the table, along with a just rinsed glass from the dish rack.

She watched Darien and he slowly poured the juice into the glass and brought it up to his lips. He took a long sip, stopped, then took another one that finished it off. At that moment Tish knew that he was finished, it was confirmed when he pushed his plate away and wiped his mouth.

"So, what did you do today?" Darien asked as he sat back in his chair.

"Just our regular Saturday routine," she replied, still chewing on her food. "Housework, laundry, and we went to the library."

"Did the girls pick out some good books?"

Tish kept her head down when she replied, "I guess so, I didn't get a chance to look through them yet." Then it was silence again, no one said a word. Darien reached for a toothpick and started cleaning his teeth. He watched as Tish finished what was left on her plate. After a few minutes, Darien broke the silence.

"It really felt good being back at work," Darien muttered. "Dutch was right, they missed me over there too.

"Was it really?" she responded.

"Workload was piled up as usual. I was trying to work, and they couldn't stop talking," Darien laughed. "They were trying to get me all caught up with the gossip and man, it was some crazy mess going on these last two years."

Tish cleared the table without responding to the last comment about his great adventure at work, she knew what was on both of their minds, and that was Tonya.

Why does he insist on playing games with me? Now he's going to sit there and deliberately withhold information that he knows I'm waiting for. He is always trying to spare my feelings by keeping things from me, but that's wrong because when that shit comes out, it blows up in his face. I do not have time for this, she thought as she cleared the kitchen table of her and Darien's dinner dishes.

Darien got up and grabbed a bottle of spring water out of the refrigerator. The sound of the chair scraping the floor when he pushed it under the table caused Tish to look back at him.

"Are you okay?" she quickly asked, looking into his eyes searching for clues, as if his eyes were a screen that recorded everything that occurred today.

Sure, I am, why do you ask?" He walked over to her, avoiding looking her into her eyes. He gave her a light peck on the cheek, "I'll meet you in the bedroom. It's been a long day and I'm tired, very tired."

Tish watched him walk away from her and out of the kitchen before she made gestures in the air with her face.

"Damn, damn, damn!" she stomped on the kitchen floor cussing to herself, trying to figure out what the big secret was. *He already told me he was over there. I think it's very selfish of him not to even let me know how his sister was doing. Oh, maybe she told him that I hadn't tried to contact her or stop by her house to see if she was alright, but she's a big girl, she don't need a babysitter.*

Besides, she don't like me anyway.

Tish leaned over the kitchen sink while suds ran down each plate. As she slowly wiped each dish with a cloth, she thought about going back to the old neighborhood to get her little package. After that, she'd sit in front of the TV with her *Pepsi* and large bag of potato chips, watching a good movie and just calling it an evening. She felt that it was the only way to relax herself, to forget about what was going on around her that caused her pain.

When I am turned on the world is beautiful. I'm happy, carefree and relaxed, Darien loves me, and I love him. There is no Tonya. She does not exist. Just me, Darien and my girls living a happy life.

Tish was a frequent user, but it did not interfere with the care and upkeep of her family and home. Hiding her using was actually band aids, used to cover up the pain.

Tish continued to clean the kitchen, putting away condiments, wiping the stove off. All she could think about was ways to get Darien to open up.

After she swept the kitchen floor and got up the trash, she placed the broom into the kitchen closet. Just as she was about to reach for the light switch to turn it off, she just so happened to see a light come on in Khalif's apartment. She watched as he moved around, looking from room to room. When she saw the steam coming from the bathroom window,

and the blinds going down, she moved away from the window, turning off the kitchen light to join Darien in the bedroom. She was very careful not to make any noise as she undressed.

Once she noticed that Darien was apparently asleep, she carefully slid into bed and slowly covered herself up to her shoulders while turning her back to Darien.

"Are you asleep?" whispered Darien, along with a light tap on her shoulder. She just laid there, wondering why he waited so long to say something. She had just started dozing off and didn't want to come out of it.

She mumbled, "Why? You need something?" She lifted her head slightly in the darkness.

"Regina says hello," Darien said quickly.

Oh no, he did not do that to me, Tish thought to herself. *How's he gonna wake me up with this when he had all evening to tell me. It has been a long day for me, and I have a feeling it's going to be a long night. Let the shit show begin.*

She slowly rolled over on her side to look into his sleepy, glaring eyes, waiting for a response.

"How about Tonya?" she raised an eyebrow back to him before cringing. *I could kick myself in the butt for asking that question, it just slipped out. Oh well, the way those eyes are jumping around right now tells me this conversation is going to go on till the morning.*

"Tonya is good," said Darien, rolling onto his back, taking most of the cover with him. "She put on a little weight. As far as I know, she seems to be doing okay. What made you think she was there?"

Tish roughly tried to take the cover back, "I heard she's always there. Even when she had her own apartment, she was right there at Regina's house."

"Oh, so you've been talking to Regina then?" he questioned, pulling himself up to a sitting position.

"Oh no I didn't talk to 'Gina, and I haven't been by there either," she snapped.

"Yeah, that was exactly what she said too"

"So, what did you guys talk about Darien?"

"Regina's new job at Livingston mall. Mainly she mentioned something about some man she just broke up with, and how much he wanted to be all over her all the time, but whenever she needed some help, he would disappear until he knew she had money."

"Regina should know better. She don't know it's either the money or the man? Seems like you can't have both."

"And you say that to say what, Tish?"

Tish was starting to reach a boiling point. She couldn't understand why Darien was holding back telling her about Tonya's new residence.

She needs him to know that these are some of the things that make her think there's something going on between the two of them.

"Darien, I called Regina today. I got an answer, but she couldn't come to the phone so she's right as far as she knows. Apparently, Tonya didn't give her my message."

"Oh, so you know she stayed there then."

"Yes, I know," she scoffed, turning her back to Darien. "I'm going to sleep. We'll talk in the morning. I'm tired."

He didn't say a word, laying on his back, hands folded behind his head, staring into the darkness until he fell asleep.

Tish couldn't sleep, she wanted desperately to make a quick run. There was a battle going on in her head on whether to get up and go for it or take a chance of failing a drug test when the time came to be hired. *I'll just lay here and feel through it* she tried to clear her head, but the words "I live here now" kept repeating over and over. Tish reached for her cell phone on the nightstand, tapped the music icon, and then put her earplugs in. She listened to the music for about an hour or so until she felt her head was clear enough to fall off to sleep. She set an alarm for 6 AM, then plugged her phone up to charge overnight. Listening to the sounds of Darien snoring finished her off, and she was fast asleep with her head under the cover.

Chapter 8

Sunday morning breakfast was done and ready to eat when Tish woke up, it was actually the smell of the bacon that popped her eyes open. She climbed out of bed and made her way to the bathroom. It was like the smell of bacon was pulling her by the nose when she entered the kitchen. Darien and the girls were already seated, gorging on pancakes, sausages, bacon, and eggs like one was going to take more than the other.

“Slow down some guys, I want to eat too,” Tish said.

“It’s plenty here Mom, Dad really cooked a lot this morning. He must’ve worked up an appetite yesterday,” Shakima teased.

“I don’t know about that, Shakima. He didn’t finish his dinner last night.”

Darien intentionally made a noise clearing his throat, “I’m not invisible, ladies.”

"Why did you say that, Daddy?" Rahanna asked, before she stuffed her mouth with a piece of a syrup covered pancake.

"They're talking like I'm not even here. Yes, I did work up an appetite and I couldn't finish my food because I was too tired to even eat."

"Well, you're making up for it right now, that's for sure." They all laughed, and Tish started fixing her plate.

They laid around resting and watching television for the rest of the day. Darien watched sports in the living room, while the girls listened to music and played video games. They all met up in the kitchen later for a late lunch/early dinner, chatting a little, before returning to their entertainment corners. Tish spent most of her day going over some data programs and reading the books she checked out of the library yesterday.

The thought of Tonya occasionally entered her head, but she decided not to mention her to Darien, not today anyways. The day was going too smooth and quiet for them to get back on that subject. Since Darien hadn't mentioned anything about her, she felt it was like that for now, but they both knew what was on each other's minds. Whatever's going on, they both knew that it had to be resolved before they were to go over to Regina's house together.

"Dutch is not picking me up tomorrow, I'm going to need the car," Darien said calmly as he rested in front of the television in his brown leather recliner. Tish had just walked into the living room to sit down and relax for a while before turning in for the night.

"I don't have anywhere to go tomorrow, so you can take the car Darien."

"Regina asked me to take her to work in the morning. She started a new job."

"What kind of job?"

"Shoe store at the Livingston mall, she's being hired as a manager."

"Good for her." As the evening came to an end, everyone said good night and went to their bedrooms.

The next morning, Tish woke to an empty house. Darien and the girls had already left. Tish had some breakfast, showered, and dressed before she headed out the door to start her day. She waved to a neighbor as she passed him on the street. She aimlessly walked over blocks before stopping at a store to purchase some items for dinner. She took another route on her way back, she wanted to see what the front of Khalif's house looked like. She noticed how beautiful the one- and two-family houses were on the block. She felt proud of her new neighborhood and hoped that one day soon she'd get to converse with her new neighbors.

As she walked with her mind on Darien and Tonya, she accidentally bumped into a man on the sidewalk. He was just stepping off his porch when they both collided, the groceries flew out of the bag and onto the hot pavement. She started gathering up the scattered food, apologizing frivolously without looking up

"You weren't just walking around, not paying attention. Something led you here." The voice sounded familiar.

"Excuse me, sir," Tish said, while slowly coming up to a standing position to meet the familiar voice. "Khalif! Oh, my goodness, is that you?"

"Yes, it's me alright. I was wondering when you were going to make your way around here," he chuckled. "How are you, Tish?"

"I'm good, Khalif, how have you been?"

"It's going, it's going, I can't complain," Khalif shrugged. "Where are you headed to?"

"I was just out to get a few things for dinner, and I decided to take the longer way back, to get some air, ya know?" Khalif laughed, and she couldn't help but laugh as well.

"Oh yeah," he said nodding. "I do know."

They both reached their arms out to give each other a hug, "How's the girls, Tish?"

"They're doing fine, thanks for asking. And what about your son, how is he doing?"

"He's great, no problem."

"Is he still with you?"

"No, he's living with his mother now..." Khalif looked down.

"Oh." Tish muttered awkwardly.

"It's okay, he was going through something without her. He missed her terribly."

"I know it must've been hard for you to let him go back to his mom," Tish said, looking him in the eye.

"It was, because I got used to having him around, someone to take care of, someone to talk to. I mean, we talk on the phone a lot now though, it's something," He shook his head. "So, what have you been doing with yourself these last two years?"

"Family and school, school and family, that's pretty much it."

"School?" he asked. "So, you did get into real estate. Great, that's fabulous."

"Yeah, I have one more month to go."

"That's wonderful! This calls for a celebration," Khalif winked.

"But I'm not finished yet," Tish laughed.

"That's alright, we can celebrate anyway. Who knows the next time we'll see each other again."

"You're right, I really had a nice chat with you that day we jumped over the fence." They both laughed.

"Your husband, um, Dan...?"

"You mean Darien, he's fine. Went MIA for two years, but that's a whole 'nother chapter." Tish shook her head.

"Two years," Khalif raised his eyebrows in disbelief. "And where were you all that time?"

"Right around the corner, believe it or not." Tish looked at her groceries and then at her watch. She didn't want to walk away from Khalif. She felt she needed someone to talk to, Khalif stopped her from doing something she didn't want to do. She was only a few blocks from getting her fix then she would've been in the world of no worries.

"Okay, I have until 3:30, the girls are at summer camp and they'll be home by then. That's more than enough time. I need to get some things from the store, we can walk or take my car."

"Why don't we just use what I have here? What do you say?"

"I'm all in," Tish smiled. She followed Khalif up the brick-paved steps and through a large, heavy wood door that led to a narrow hallway.

"Just one flight up," he mentioned.

"I know," Tish said before her eyes widened.

"You what?" He turned to look at her, confused.

"Oh, I said 'that's all'?"

Inside Khalif's apartment Tish looked around at the art on the walls. "You have a nice place, how long have you been here?"

"Too long, I can't remember," Khalif shook his head, chuckling.

"Do you like it here?" she asked.

"Sure, it's okay. Well, you know, I would like to own my own home one day. Before I get too old to enjoy it."

"Please, most people do get a chance to enjoy their home, why do you say that?"

"Because you're working every day, sometimes overtime, and when you get home all you want to do is sleep. Then as soon as you wake up it's time to go back to work again. All you need is one room and a TV; the TV will put you to sleep." They both laughed.

They were standing by the window at this point, looking over his apartment.

"So, I guess that's your husband I see sometimes in the kitchen cooking," Khalif said.

"Have you been spying on us, Mr. Khalif?"

"Ha ha," he chuckled. "No, not really, I was actually looking for you."

"Yeah, Darien gets up and fixes breakfast for us sometimes. He likes to cook, and because he goes to bed so early, he usually gets up before I do."

"I'm an early bird myself, I don't like sleeping late hours like I used to. I hate that tired feeling going into work, so my lights are out usually around 9:30 or so."

"Yes, I've noticed." The words slipped out before she could catch them. Khalif looked at her with squinting eyes.

"Have you been spying on me, Miss Tish?" They both let out a big laugh.

"Put some music on Khalif, I have to get this food cooking so we can get the celebration started up in here!"

He stood there, smiling at first, just watching her try to find her way around his kitchen. He really admired the way she dressed, her body structure, and her movement. He noticed it all the first day he saw her.

"Come on, put on some soft music, some jazz instrumental, and light an incense. That's sandalwood, I love it." He looked over at her and nodded his head "yes".

Khalif started picking up some things he had lying around the apartment: some shirts, a few jackets, books, and started putting them in their right place. He looked over at Tish from time to time, and when he felt the time was right, he would interrupt by showing her a picture or two of his son, his mom and his sisters. He really enjoyed having a woman around the house. It's been a long time since he and his wife parted, the feel of a woman cooking for him again boosted his spirits. *A woman like Tish, she is all I could ever ask for,* he thought.

He poured them both a glass of red wine and handed one to Tish. She smiled, took a sip, and went back to cooking. Tish, out of nowhere, let out a big laugh, almost choking on her wine.

"Oh no," she said out loud." It's so crazy."

"What's so crazy?" Khalif asked, looking around the kitchen like whatever it was had something to do with the food.

She was still laughing. "I have to stop at the store on my way home to buy the same thing and cook it again," she snickered. "But it's okay. I don't mind, it's just so funny to even think about it."

"You need to be in the restaurant business," he said, joining her in laughter.

Khalif was still laughing when his phone rang. He put his ear to the device, holding a finger up to Tish with a *wait a second* when he noticed she was about to speak. Khalif was talking to the caller for a few minutes when, all of a sudden, his smile dropped. He then disconnected the call and sat with a blank stare, not saying a word.

"Bad news?" Tish asked

When he failed to respond, Tish left him to his deep thoughts to go finish up in the kitchen.

What the heck was that all about? she thought to herself while cleaning up the finished meal. *He looked like he just saw a ghost or something. What could have possibly been said to him to make him go from cracking up laughing to looking like his world just ended. I hope everything's alright with his son.*

Tish walked over to the coffee table and placed both plates in the center, near the wine.

Khalif stood up and reached inside of a white candle holder to grab a lighter. He lit the two candles that were on the table, still silent. Tish noticed that his movements were different, it was like his whole demeanor had changed.

She went into her head, *Is this man psychotic? Who the hell just changes their whole attitude like that, especially when they have company? Who the hell was that on the phone? This feels strange. I'm locked in this house with a man I really don't know, he gets a call and starts acting weird, is the caller on their way here?*

She looked over at the front door, there were several locks. She thought about how she was going to get them all undone before she was grabbed. *And I don't think the candles are appropriate, this was not supposed to be a romantic dinner. Did I give him the wrong impression? I just needed someone to talk to.* She felt strange and wanted to leave.

Khalif finally broke his silence, "Wow, this looks good. Chicken parmesan, asparagus, and my favorite, yellow rice. It smells wonderful, Tish."

Tish was thoroughly confused.

They ate quietly for a few minutes before he spoke once more, "That was a friend of mine, Bobby, who I just spoke to on the phone. He said he was about to go into rehab and needed a place to stay when he got out. We go way back, did a lot of things together, but I'm not about that life anymore. I had to let him go. Some people learn then some people learn the hard way. You know what I mean, Tish?"

Tish just sat there, staring.

"What's the problem, woman?" he asked. "What? You thought I was a masked murderer or something? Coming up to kill you?"

He laughed out loud, "You thought we were both going to do you in, ha."

"No, I didn't, Khalif."

"Yes, you did." She started laughing.

He put his arms around her, “I don’t want him to come here, and if I ignore him, he’ll find someone else to go to.”

“Is he *that* bad?” Tish asked.

“He’s really that bad.”

“Oh, I see.”

Khalif straightened to further explain, “It’s just that he’s always in and out, never getting his life together. I gave him too many chances. We’ve been friends for as long as I can remember, and he’s still the same selfish, freeloading bastard.”

He then shakes his head, “Let’s forget him, I don’t want to talk about that.

I have this beautiful woman sitting with me along with a delicious meal and some wine, I don’t want to spoil it on someone who don’t even care about himself.”

He lifted his wine glass to toast; Tish did the same.

“Here’s to your real estate career!”

“Thank you so much, Khalif,” Tish smiled.

Khalif cleared the table once they finished eating. They decided to sit on the wine and listen to music. Tish was beginning to feel comfortable with him, so comfortable that she wanted to tell him about the situation with her and Darien.

She thought he could maybe tell her something that might help She was beginning to feel a little tipsy, and refused a third glass of wine, “I’ve had enough, Khalif, I just want to talk to you about something that’s been bothering me and I’m not sure how to handle it.”

She then explained to him how she felt about Darien spending so much time with Tonya, and how much it was interfering with their relationship. As she talked Khalif could hear the tension surfacing in her voice. In an effort to make her smile again, he decided to stop her and try to change the direction of the conversation.

"Tish, there is no doubt in my mind that this man loves you. Some men just have a strange way of dealing with family life. I feel this woman is just a friend to him. Now, I think you should just trust that until you have some concrete proof."

"That's the part I don't like about this, Khalif, there's always this doubt; And he's not showing me at all that he's trying to satisfy it, regardless of me telling him what's bothering me. And why does he ignore me?" She takes a breath before looking down. "I think I'm talking too much."

"No, no, it's alright," reassured Khalif. "Hey, I just want you to know that, personally, I don't think he would do anything to jeopardize his relationship with his wife and kids, coming from a man's point of view. He's got it all, he's a lucky man and he knows this."

Khalif looked at his watch then turned on the TV, putting the remote control next to Tish.

The moment quickly turned awkward when they looked up to see a couple on the screen aggressively kissing and pulling off their clothes. Khalif cleared his throat and hurriedly reached for the remote, but Tish beat him to it. They both took a deep breath and relaxed as Tish flipped through the channels.

"I have about two hours before the girls get out of day camp. I guess I better head back home, you know I have to cook. I really had a nice time here, Khalif. I'm going to put your number in my cell for the next time I need a friend to talk to."

Khalif took the remote control out of her hand and turned the TV off before shifting his body to face her.

"Tish," he said while looking her straight in the eyes, "I've been dreaming about a woman like you. Your personality, your character, the way you carry yourself is exactly what I dream about. I'm not settling until I find that woman and if Darien ever-"

"No, don't say it, my friend," she sighs, placing her hand over his. "Now, you are so sweet, we're going to *be friends* and we're going to be just fine. I can feel it. On that note, I've gotta go!"

Khalif grabbed her hand to help her stand to her feet. Tish tried hard not to look him in the eyes. She was unsure of what she was feeling, but she had a good idea of what was on his mind.

Khalif walked her to the door.

"I'll call you," she sighs, walking into the hallway. She still didn't look him in the eyes.

"Oh, Tish, congratulations on your new job, and please don't be a-"

"Oh, I sure won't. You're in my contacts list, my friend," She laughs, leaving out the door.

"Alright, you take care."

"You too!" Tish too down the stairs. When she reached the bottom, she looked up at Kelis door. It was closed. She walked out to the front porch, closing the big heavy door behind her.

Tish looked up and down the street before stepping off the porch. The sunlight caused her to rub her a bit, it took a minute before she regained her eyesight. As she walked away from the house, she looked up at Khalif's window, and just as she suspected, he was looking back.

She waved. He waved back. She turned and kept walking.

Lord God, what am I feeling? Why do I have this big smile on my face? Okay, so I'm going to take it as unloading stress through good conversation, and that's all. She had to laugh to herself, because subconsciously she knew that was not the truth. *I had to stop him in his tracks because I knew where it was heading. Things just can't be like that, not now. I'm trying to work on saving my marriage. I hope he got that message...*

The grocer gave Tish a hard stare when she ordered the same things and placed the same items on the counter. When she noticed he was about to ask about it, she just held her hand up, "Don't ask, it's a long story."

He shook his head and let Tish pay him before she walked out of the store.

That night at dinner the girls asked to be excused to work on a project for summer camp which left Tish and Darien alone in their silence. They were both in deep thought, not even a glance was shared between the two. Darien looked tired as always, Tish knew his next move was straight to the bedroom and to bed.

It was the sound of the landline phone ringing that broke them from their trance. Tish stood up to answer it.

"Yes sis, it has been a long time. What have you been up to? You must have been very busy."

"You couldn't give your big sis a call? When're you coming here?"

Darien looked up at Tish.

"Okay, I'll meet you at the train station at 2. Alright, bye."

Tish sat back down at the kitchen table to finish her dinner, Darien then got up and dropped the remains of his food into the garbage bin.

He put his plate in the sink and stood there, watching the running water cascade down the surface. Tish should've noticed that he didn't have his work boots on. She didn't see him when he left that morning, but she knew he always wore his boots to work. That was an invitation for a conversation, she was curious about the switch.

"Where are your boots, Darien?" She asked him.

"Where are my what?" He answered, raising a brow.

"Your boots, why do you have sneakers on?"

"Oh, I didn't want to bring those muddy things in the house. I put them in the basement and walked upstairs with just my socks on."

"I don't see the need for you to put sneakers on to walk around the house."

"Damn," Darien was beginning to get annoyed and didn't feel like answering Tish, so, he started doing the questioning. "How long is she staying? Your sister, I mean."

"She didn't say, I'm going to have to drop you off at work so I can pick her up from the train station."

"Alright, what did you do today?" He asked.

"Not much, just some shopping and cleaning, my usual," She shrugged.

"But I smell alcohol, have you been drinking?"

The question made Tish pause. When she came home early that day the first thing she did was brush her teeth and gargle with mouth wash. Usually, whenever Darien smelled alcohol, he knew there were drugs involved. Tish didn't want him to think she was back using, so she tried to change the topic.

"Do you think Dutch could pick you up from work or do you need me to do it?"

"I'll call him and ask him, I'll let you know before you go to bed."

Tis cleaned the kitchen, put the dishes away, mopped the floor, and set the garbage in the hall for Darien to take down in the morning. The house was quiet, the girls were in bed. She made herself a glass of ice water with half a lemon squeezed into it, drinking it straight down. She took the glass over to the sink to rinse it out and placed it in the dish rack.

Tish was not surprised at all when she looked up to see Khalif waving to her from the window. She smiled and waved back before turning the kitchen light off, noticing he did the same. She went to the bedroom and started to undress.

Tish paused when she looked down and saw a leather strap sticking out from under the bed. She pulled it out. The strap was attached to a leather briefcase, she slowly pulled it from under the bed without disturbing Darien. It was unzipped with a few folders and loose papers. There was another compartment that was filled with letters addressed and opened.

She carefully placed the letters back that fell out of the bag while noticing they were addressed to the correctional facility. Tish put the strap over her shoulder, walked out of the bedroom and hurried into the bathroom. She pulled out at least five letters, sitting on the stool to observe the sender's name one by one.

They were all sent by Tonya.

Tonya Smith, Tonya Smith, Tonya Smith, Tonya Smith. Tears started to fall, her eyes turning cloudy with a lump in her throat. Suddenly, it was hard to swallow, her heart beating fast. She just could not believe what she was reading. An hour had passed of sitting in the bathroom reading letter after letter before she stormed out of the bathroom yelling, not caring about waking the girls up. She was hurt.

Her suspicions were right, and she had to get answers. She yelled louder as she stomped through the hall towards the bedroom.

"Darien! Darien, she's been writing you!" Tish yelled, pulling the covers off him and throwing them to the floor. He shifted his body to face her, eyes squinting as they tried to adjust to the light.

"What's wrong with you, woman? I was asleep! What are you waking me up for?"

"She's been writing to you all this time," Tish seethed, barely getting the words out. Herr chest hurt, so much that she wanted to go to the hospital because it pain was almost unbearable. "You are such a liar. You are such a *liar,* Darien! I trusted and believed in you for so long, and when I had my doubts, I kept it to myself because I didn't want to destroy what we had."

Darien got up off the bed, "Tish, hold on a minute, you are not being rational right now. I need you to listen to me please-"

"Listen to what, Darien, to what?" She was beyond angry. She walked over to the side of his bed, throwing everything in her way across the room. Tish then looked him in the eyes. "Do you think I had these girls so they could grow up to be fatherless? Wouldn't that be sick?"

She was still yelling, "Did you think that once I found out the truth, I would still stay with you?"

"Calm down Tish, you're going to say something that you don't mean."

"I'm not calming down, I want answers, and I want them tonight, Darien!"

Darien sat back on the bed and took a deep breath. He tried to think back to anything that could have made her so suspicious of Tonya. He couldn't think of anything. He'd been trying his best to keep the two of them apart, he felt that after all this time he had been doing a good job.

The harder I try to keep Tish away and content the worse it gets. I can't tell her Tonya needs me and depends on me during this storm in her life. Sure, she had men in her life after we broke up. Plenty for that matter, but there was no one for her to go to when she needed moral support and sometimes financial support. Tish would never understand that she's living with Regina because her last boyfriend stepped out on her, leaving her with a four month past due mortgage bill, a $900 phone bill, and maxed out credit card.

Tonya doesn't want to cause trouble between Tish and I, she has proven that to me time after time. Despite that, I know she would love to have me back in her life full time, I can tell when we're together. She surrenders, holding me tight like she never wants to let me go, but my family is my life. I would be there for Tonya, but she understands that I need to be with my babies and that means I have to be with Tish.

Darien sat Tish down on the edge of the bed, not taking his eyes off her. He calmly tried to get through to her. He didn't want the girls to hear what was being said, not wanting to upset them.

"All those letters are just something to read, that's all. They mean nothing to me, Tish, do you hear me?"

"You said there was nothing going on. I asked you because I wanted to be clear about this. You said you were just friends."

"Those letters don't prove anything; they were just something to read. Believe me, Tish."

She picked up one of the letters and read it to Darien, "'See you soon, love.'"

She threw it down onto the bed and picked up another one, "'Wish our visit could have lasted longer.' Dated one month ago!" She threw it at him and picked up another one.

"Stop Tish, come on, come to bed. It's getting late and you are making too much noise."

"This is the reason why you spent so much time at your sister's house. She wrote in this letter that she couldn't wait to get you into her arms again, do you think I'm some kind of fool?"

Hearing those words come out of Tish's mouth crushed Darien's heart. He knew how much Tish loved him and believed in him, he never wanted to hurt her.

Tish couldn't stop crying, "I want to believe, Darien, I needed to believe you."

She hurried into the living room and threw herself onto the sofa, Darien soon followed to console her.

He put his arms around her shoulders, "Forget about those letters, it'll be the two of us together with the girls as a family forever." Those were the words she needed to hear, the ones she had been waiting for ever since he came home, they were finally said.

For the next hour or so Tish surrendered to Darien like it was the first day of their marriage, she wanted so badly to believe him. She wanted to believe that one day Darien would start staying home and spending more time with her and the girls. She hoped he would leave Regina to work out her own issues, and that Tonya just would disappear entirely.

Chapter 9

Tish opened her eyes to the morning sun practically blinding her. She made her way to the bathroom to bathe, brush her teeth and then started breakfast. Darien was the first to enter the kitchen and the girls followed suit.

"Good morning, Mom," yawned Rahanna.

"Good morning to you too, sweetie, did you sleep well?"

"Yes ma'am, I did," she responded.

"How did you sleep, Mom?" asked Shakima.

"I slept well, Kima, and you?"

"I heard you crying, that's why I asked. Why were you crying?"

"Come on girls, eat so we can get out of here. I don't want to be late," Darien intervened, looking over at Tish. She felt his gaze but didn't return the look. She was standing at the kitchen window, sipping on her coffee when they left the kitchen to get ready. Tish stared at Khalif's window hoping she could catch a glance of him before he left for work.

The ride to the girls' school was quiet, except for the low sounds coming from the game Rahanna was playing. Darien stared out the window, not saying a word until the girls were out of the car.

"You know we can't keep going on like this, Darien," Tish said, breaking the silence.

"See, this is what I mean about you. We work things out and make up and everything, then there you go bringing things up again. That's why we can't work nothing out."

"Darien, what happened last night was *not* working things out, it was just something we both needed from each other. It did not solve anything."

"So, what do you want me to do Tish? Tell me, what do you want me to do?"

Tish didn't say a word as she pulled up at his job. She parked the car and sat there, waiting for him to get out.

"We'll talk tonight when I get off," Darien sighed before he closed the door and walked off.

An hour or so later Tish met up with her sister, Patricia. After they embraced, Patricia got into the car and went straight into sister-girlfriend mode. They asked each other billions of questions and laughed the entire way back to the house.

"It's so much fun talking about the good old times," Patricia said while looking over at Tish, smiling. "I really missed you, sis, couldn't wait to get here. Kirkwood, Georgia is just not the same without you."

"Same here, little sis," Tish nodded, looking up at Khalif's window when she passed the house. "How's mom?"

Patricia couldn't help but notice the dryness in her voice, it was like she had to force herself to ask.

"She's doing good, she asks about you all the time. Sis, why don't you call her? She would love to hear from you. When was the last time you two talked?"

"It's been a while, but you know how we get along. We always get into a big argument when we talk to each other or when we see each other. I don't need all that right now."

"She means well, she misses you too."

"To her, everything I do is wrong. Even if I do something right, she doesn't acknowledge it, she'd never give me credit for what I do. She puts too much emphasis on what I *don't* do. Don't get me wrong, I love mama dearly, but I just have to love her from a distance. That's the only way."

They pulled up in front of the house and Tish helped Patricia get her luggage upstairs. Once inside, Tish led her to the girls' room and told her that that's where she would be sleeping. They unpacked her things and made room for some of her clothes to hang in the closet.

"How are you and Darien doing?" Patricia asked, putting the last shirt on a hanger.

"We're not," Tish shrugged.

"What do you mean by that?" Her sister questioned as she flopped down on the bed, joining Tish.

"He's seeing someone." Patricia looked at her in disbelief, beyond shocked at what she was hearing.

"You're lying. Tish, don't say that, why are you saying that?" She shook her head.

"Because it's true. You remember the girl I wrote to you about? The one he was dating before me?"

"Yeah, I remember her. Wow, Tonya?"

"If you ask me, I think they never stopped seeing each other."

"I don't believe that" said Patricia, shaking her head from side to side.

"Sis, you know how I feel about my marriage and my family, this is something I wouldn't ever joke about. Plus, I found some letters last night," said Tish, looking straight into Patricia's eyes as hers began to tear up.

"Tish, I'm so sorry, this is terrible."

"I agree," nodded Tish.

"You guys have to talk this out, there's too much at stake here. I mean, you know, what about the girls, do they know?"

"No not yet, but Shakima knows there's something wrong."

"Why do you say that?"

"She heard me crying last night, and she knew that I slept on the couch."

"Poor baby, it's so hard for kids to understand things like this, it's so sad. He's such a good provider, he loves his family, Tish, I know he does. There must be some misunderstanding here."

"So, you're telling me I'm making it all up?"

"You have to be, you know how your imagination can fly away sometimes," Patricia sighed,

"Well, let me tell you something, sister dear," she said while getting off the bed, turning her head with her hands on her hips. "Letters don't lie."

Tish walked out of the room, leaving her sister alone. After a few minutes, she returned with the letters and threw them on the bed. "I'm going to start dinner and make some lunch. You tell me what you can make out of this."

Tish opened the refrigerator door and reached for the packaged sliced turkey, provolone cheese, and some horseradish, mustard and butter. She melted some butter in a pan, cut two rolls in half, browned them on the open side, and placed the turkey and cheese on top. She finished the sandwiches then went back into the refrigerator for two yogurts, mixing her favorite ingredients into one of the containers. She was pouring iced tea when Patricia walked in, taking a seat at the table.

"It seems to me that something is going on. Based off these letters, you are not imagining anything, sis."

"That's what I've been trying to tell you. Darien told me to forget about the letters and that everything is gonna be alright. He said we could break up and maybe get a divorce, but nobody would end up happy."

"And what did he mean by that?"

"Girl, I don't know." They both laughed

"Sister, I think I came to visit at the wrong time," Patricia sighed sadly, shaking her head.

"Patty, I need you here, you came at the right time. I need you to give me some real talk before I do something that's going to affect our lives. Besides, there's nothing like having a sister to talk to when you're going through tough times. I'm glad you're here."

"Me too. Come on, let's finish eating so we can cook dinner together."

They worked around the kitchen gathering ingredients. With Tish showing Patricia her recipes, and Patricia doing the same, dinner was done in no time. Patricia put the lid on the smothered turkey chops and took the mac & cheese out of the oven. Tish turned off the asparagus and let it rest in the olive oil and fresh garlic.

Patricia started laughing, "Tish, remember when Mom would always prepare baked turkey with big potatoes? It was so good; we couldn't stay out of the pan."

Tish burst into laughter, "Boy, do I remember those days. She caught me one day sneaking into the pan after we had dinner. She yelled at me so loud, 'Are you trying to eat all the food up from your dad?' And the funny thing is, she never realized how much was missing until she caught us!"

They sat at the kitchen table talking until the girls came home from summer camp. When they heard the key turning, they just sat quietly, eyeing the door to see the girls' expression when they laid their eyes on their auntie.

Their faces were empty and tired when they walked through the door. Shakima was the first to notice them sitting at the kitchen table when she turned from struggling to get the key out of the lock. She dropped everything: her book bag, laptop, and keys on the floor. Rahanna followed suit. Tish had to save them from falling over as they made their way to the kitchen.

"Oh girls, you just don't know how happy I am to see you!"

"Well, it had been a long time, Auntie," said Shakima.

“Yes, it has been, look at how much you have grown young lady! And I love what you girls did with your room, simply beautiful, so much character!”

Tish gave them a few minutes more before sending them to their room to change. Patricia was about to follow the girls until she stopped her. Tish leaned over towards her so that the girls wouldn’t hear her.

“What we talked about today, sis, keep it hush. Don’t even say anything to Darien. You got it?”

“Yes, I’ve got it, my mouth is shut.”

“Thanks Patty. I need to step out for a while to pick up Darien from work.”

“Sure, go ahead, just leave it to me to finish up here. You just go.”

Tish rushed out of the kitchen, looking back at Patricia, “Thanks sis, I won’t be gone long.”

She hurried to the bathroom to wash her face and hands and noticed she didn’t have her wedding ring on. She looked on the counter, in the sink, down on the floor, in the toilet, and, with wet hands, she searched her pockets. Nothing. Tish panicked as she rushed into the kitchen, scanning every inch of the room, saying nothing to Patricia. She became a nervous wreck at the thought of losing her wedding ring. She also knew for a fact that there was no way it could have slipped off her finger between Khalif’s house and hers. It was too much of a perfect fit for that. She had a strong feeling the ring was at Khalif’s and decided to go there first before picking Darien up from work.

Tish thought back to when she was in the kitchen cooking. She believes she took her rings off to clean the chicken. That’s something she usually does on the regular.

She parked the car a few houses away from Khalif's house. Tish looked up at the open window before entering the building. She hurried up the stairs and stood at the door for a few seconds to catch her breath before knocking. Khalid answered right away, thinking it was someone else. He was amazed to see Tish standing at the door, though, by his reaction, she knew he was expecting someone else. He welcomed her in and told her to have a seat.

"How are you?" He asked. "I'm surprised to see you so soon."

"Yeah, I'm surprised to be here so soon."

"Is everything okay?"

"No, I'm a nervous wreck right now Khalif."

"Why, what happened?" He looked concerned.

"My rings, Khalif I lost my rings. I think they're here. I hope they're here."

"Oh no, that's not good," he said looking around the living room. "Feel free to look around with me. You checked your car good?"

"I sure did," Tish said, nodding her head.

"I'll check the kitchen; I haven't cooked anything since you left. Things are pretty much untouched," Khalif said as he entered the kitchen.

"Ah ha!!" he yelled, dancing his way back into the living room and over to Tish, grabbing her hand. He led her into a few dance moves, spun her around and bowed. "You will be happy to know that your rings were safely resting on my kitchen soap dish, waiting for your return, my lady"

"You are so funny, Khalif. I knew they were here," Tish sighed in relief.

He took her hand while looking her in the eyes. She tried hard not to lock eyes with him but soon gave in. She felt him slowly placing the rings on, sliding it in its right place. He gently pushed her away to resist the temptation of kissing her hand.

"Tish, I really enjoyed you being here with me. Cooking, talking, listening to music, it's something I haven't done in a long time. I'm not saying I haven't been dating, don't get me wrong, there have been women in my life. But with you, it's different. I feel like I've known you all my life."

"I had a nice time with you too, Khalif, but I don't know where we're going with this. You know my situation. What I'm trying to say is, we just can't do this."

She walked away from him and sat by the window; he followed her. "I found letters."

"You found letters," he repeated. "What kind of letters?"

"It's a long story, so much has happened since the day we rode the bus together. Darien has been in trouble with the law. He did some time, and someone from his past was writing him letters."

"I'm so sorry to hear that, are you okay?"

"You want to know something? I'm really trying to work through this, but you're presenting a situation here that's going to make things even worse." She looked up at him. "I think I should stop coming around here for a while, just to get my head together and to straighten some things out."

"I don't see any reason why we can't be friends, Tish."

"You don't see any reason why? Well, I'm gonna tell you. When I saw the look in your eyes a moment ago, I read right through it. That's why we can't be friends."

"You saw something you felt yourself, and you are afraid of it."

"Goodbye Khalif, I have to go," Tish sighed, standing up.

He then grabs her by the arm and pulls her back, passionately kissing her on the lips. She surrendered at first before catching herself. She pushed him away and smacked him in the face as hard as she could. Khalif quickly put his hands up to his face, grabbing it and shaking his head.

"Don't you ever do that to me again!" she yelled. "You can't do that to me!"

"What are you so afraid of Tish? Yourself? Look, I'm sorry, please let me make it up to you."

Tish backed away from him, turned, and ran for the door. Khalif followed and watched her run down the stairs, fearing that he would never see her again,

Darien was waiting in front of the building when Tish drove up, she was over 30 minutes late. She noticed he had a tired, aggravated look on his face. Darien got into the car and strapped up, not saying a word. Tish didn't even notice as she had her mind on Khalif. She struggled to forgive him for what he just did, knowing the problem she already had. Why did he want to add to it?

She quickly glanced over at her finger to make sure the rings were still there. In a way, she wanted to stay but she didn't want him to come on to her like that again. She felt he disrespected her, and the anger and frustration started building up again.

Why do I let these men piss me off so much? I need to learn how to get better control over my life. The things I go through just don't make any sense.

She thought about the kiss he gave her and how she wasn't resisting at first. He was right. She was afraid of herself, and what would have happened if she didn't have to pick Darien up for work.

Chapter 10

Later that night, after dinner, Darien and Patricia spent a while talking and laughing about old times. They talked about the wedding, and how long Patricia stayed on the dance floor making everyone line dance. Darien said she was the life of the party. As they were talking Darien's cell phone rang.

It was Dutch, and he was on his way over.

Darien told Tish to fix a plate for him. They were all in the living room watching movies when Dutch rang the doorbell. He remembered Patricia right away from the wedding.

"Yeah, it's been a long time. I remember we *stayed* on the dance floor," said Dutch, sitting next to her on the sofa. "I had a lot more energy back then. I wouldn't try that now, but it was fun. And the food was terrific, where did you get the caterer from, Tish?"

"One of my friends recommended them, and you always thinking about food! Boy, your plate is on the table."

"Thank you, my dear. We'll finish this talk later, Patricia."

"No, you won't!" yelled Tish. "I don't wanna hear about it."

"What's wrong with you? Had a bad day?"

"Nothing Dutch, I'm just trying to watch this movie." Tish grumbled.

Darien was in the bedroom, changing his clothes when he heard everything that was just said. He couldn't see that Tish was still upset about those letters. He figured it might take a while before she got over it, but in the meantime, he can't have her disrespecting his friend. He made a mental note to talk to her about that.

When he finished changing, he walked into the living room and told Tish he was going down to the bar for a while with Dutch, she just nodded her head. He gave her a kiss on the forehead, walked over to the other side of the sofa, and gave Patricia a kiss on the cheek. Dutch was saying good night to Tish and Patricia while Darien checked on the girls. When Tish looked up to ask Darien what time he would be back, they were gone.

"What's on your mind?" Patricia asked, looking into her eyes with a raised eyebrow.

"What are you talking about? I'm into the movie."

"No, you're not, I can tell you're not."

"Well, I was actually thinking about going into the kitchen and getting the dishes done, but I'm so comfortable right now."

"I know that feeling. Come on, I'll give you a hand."

"No, you stay and watch the movie. I'll have it done in no time."

"We'll both have it done in double 'no time'." They laughed as they got up and walked into the kitchen.

"Dinner was good, I enjoyed it," said Patricia.

"It was only because we did it together, sis."

"You are absolutely right!" They smiled. "So, what are you going to do, Tish?"

Although she didn't want to talk about it then, Tish knew what she meant.

"I haven't thought about that. Maybe I'll give it a little more time and see what happens now that Darien is aware that I know something is going on."

The dishes were almost done. Patricia was drying them, and Tish was sweeping the floor when Patricia called her over to the window.

"Come over here a minute, I want to show you something." Patricia said as she pointed to the window across the yard. "Who is that standing there, not budging, looking like a damn ghost."

She asked again, "Who is that, Tish? You know that person?"

Tish didn't know what to say, she was stunned. "Oh, that's just someone I met in the neighborhood. No one special."

"You're lying. I always know when you're lying."

"What? Tish asked, feigning confusion.

"I said you're lying, sister dear, and I can tell. I saw you over at the window earlier too, you were standing right there, and he was standing over there all sad. Is that what's wrong with Darien? Does he know?"

"No, Darien doesn't know anything. Why would you say that? I told you about the letters, there's not a damn thing wrong with Darien, he's fine. He's been fine with this situation for God knows how long, and it seems like you've been trying to take his side all day. I'm the victim here, Pat"

"But who is this guy in the window?"

"He's nothing, don't even mention him to me again."

"Alright, I won't. Whatever you say." She threw her hands up and back down, slapping them at her side.

"Let's go out for a while, I can get a friend of mine downstairs to sit with the girls," Tish sighed.

"Okay, I feel like going out for a little while."

They got ready and one hour later, they were in the car driving around, looking for a place to get a couple of drinks. Patricia turned the car radio on and found a station that was playing some disco. Tish looked at her, shook her head, and turned it off, "I don't want to hear that right now, I'm trying to think."

"You're going to hear it when you get to where we're going 'cause that's all they're playing right now."

"Just turn it off, please," Tish pleaded.

Tish and Patricia were sitting at a nearby neighborhood lounge. Tish was working on her third glass of tequila and ginger ale. The place was crowded, the dance floor full, and Tish was feeling the music. Patricia sat next to Tish, having a conversation with a young man she had just met.

She lit a cigarette and tried to hold it in a way where she looked like she knew what she was doing. Patricia was never a smoker; she couldn't stand the taste of it. She was always trying to fit in, doing this and doing that because she thought it made her socially acceptable. When she started coughing Tish burst into laughter, begging her to put it down.

She didn't pay Tish any mind. Instead, she kept puffing. She turned her back to Tish and started talking to her new friend.

"So, what did you say your name was?" Patricia asked, moving closer, almost touching his shoulder.

"I didn't, but I'm Carlton," the man responded.

"I'm Patricia, so nice to meet you," she said while extending her hand for him to shake, looking into his eyes. "You said you've been here before, right?"

"Oh yes, several times, and friend of mine has part ownership here. I come from time to time and check the place out for a few, but this is the first time I've ran into anyone as beautiful as you."

"Thank you," Patricia said with a smile. "That was so sweet. Actually, this is my first time here."

"Is it really? How do you like it so far?"

"Yes, it is. I think I like it very much."

The conversation was going very well, Tish decided to leave them alone to join some of her friends on the other side of the club.

Patricia and Carlton danced for a few songs and when he noticed that she was getting tired, he led her away from the dance floor and over to her seat. He ordered more drinks.

Carlton asked Patricia if she would like to leave and go somewhere where they could be alone and talk, but Patricia politely refused. She didn't feel comfortable with that. At that moment, things started to change. The fun, exciting atmosphere was turning dull. They were just sitting there, listening to music, watching people on the dance floor and not talking much.

Patricia noticed he had something heavy on his mind but decided against questioning it. *I guess he's not interested anymore,* she thought to herself. She kept her eyes on the dance floor watching Tish do her thing.

At least Tish was having fun. She was happy they did decide to come out for a while.

Out of nowhere, words started coming out of Carlton's mouth, his tone very aggressive and loud. Patricia started to feel uncomfortable, motioning to get Tish's attention. People were watching them now.

"I have been nice to you all night. Why don't you want to go off to be alone with me? What, you don't enjoy my company? You acted like you did!"

All Patricia wanted him to do was to lower his voice and get away from her. She had a funny feeling that this was going to get a lot worse before it ended, judging by the look on his face.

She tried to reason with him, "Look, let me tell you something. Just because we were sitting here, having a nice conversation and feeling each other, did *not* mean it was an invitation to take off with you. You got the wrong person for that, sir. This Georgia girl doesn't play that."

"Do you think I care about where you come from? You think I bought you those drinks for nothing? Money is money where I come from. and you spent mine. Now, you're coming with me."

Patricia got up off the stool to grab her cell phone and cigarettes off and started to walk away. Carlton grabbed her by the arm and pulled her back, causing her cell phone to hit the floor and shatter into pieces.

"Oh, no, he didn't," was all that came out of her mouth before she started swinging. Patricia landed three strong punches to his chest and face before he grabbed and twisted her arm behind her back. She couldn't help but let out a loud scream that landed on Tish's ears. She rushed over to help her sister from the grip he had on her arm. She swung around while yelling out and kicked him as hard as she could, but it was the second kick that landed him on the floor, balled up in a fetal position.

"What the hell just happened?" exclaimed Patricia. Tish just continued to stand in that position, ready to kick again if he got up with more mess.

"She didn't hold up the end of her bargain, changed her mind when she had enough to drink," Carlton huffed.

"He's lying, Tish, he's telling you a big damn lie. You know me better than that. I don't know why he's saying all that, he's a psycho narcissist."

"What bargain? What bargain is he talking about? Did you promise him something, Patricia?"

The crowd began to walk away once they realized nothing else was going to happen. Carlton cautiously made his way off the floor, while watching Tish's every move.

"I didn't promise him a damn thing, he just wanted me to go off with him. He wants me to leave this place and go somewhere with him and I wasn't going to do that."

"Come on girl, let's get out of here and head home."

"You haven't seen the last of me, Patricia, you're going to get yours!" Carlton hissed.

"Man, don't you ever let my name come out of your mouth again, you hear me?"

"Come on Pat, let's go," Tish sighed.

They walked out of the lounge, got in the car, and drove around the corner to the Big M, where they knew Darien and Dutch were. Tish told her to sit in the chair while she ran in rea l quick to tell Darien what just went down in the lounge.

When Tish opened the door and stepped inside, the first person she saw was Darien sitting at the bar with his back facing the door. Her heart sunk to the bottom of her stomach as she walked closer to him, trembling at the sight of his hand resting on the lap of another woman. As she got closer, and was now standing behind him, she eyed the woman with rage. Noticing Tish, the woman quickly stood up, causing Darien's hand to fall to his side.

"What's up, Tish?" said Tonya, looking very nervous, patting her hair back in place.

"You seem to be looking very nervous right now," Tish seethes with raised eyebrows.

"What the heck," mumbled Darien as he turned around, not believing it was Tish. All he remembered was leaving her at home.

Tish was too upset to speak. *After what they spoke about in the letters,* she thought *I thought that maybe it would be a while before they were back at it again.*

Darien was at a loss for words, he motioned for Tish to come towards the bar. He asked the bartender to fix the two some rum and coke on ice before standing up. He looked around the bar and yelled for Dutch to take Tonya home.

"Why are you so quiet?" He asked his wife.

"You got a lotta shit with you, Darien. This is what I sit at home all the time for?" The bartender set the drinks on the bar and took the $20 bill Darien placed for her.

"I'm not staying, Patricia is in the car I have to get home. Some mess happened with her and some pervert at the lounge, and I had to pull out some karate skills on him."

"Damn, yeah okay what'd the dude look like? I know just about everybody who hangs in there."

"We're okay, he's not a regular, but he knows one of your friends who's a co-owner."

"That's all I need to know, we've got this." Darien said, standing up. "Come on, I'll walk you to the car."

"No, it's okay, you stay right here with Tonya. I'm quite sure y'all came here together so you might as well leave together. You can take *her* home."

Tish turned and walked away, not even giving Tonya a second glance.

She jumped in the car, started it up and took off. Tish parked the car a block from the house and told Patricia she'd be right back. She ran into a brick building that looked like it was about to fall apart. Patricia watched her go in and waited for what seemed like hours for her to come back out.

When she did return, she was different. Her voice was slurred, she seemed a lot happier and was singing to the music that played on the radio, which was strange because she wanted it off earlier. Patricia watched her as she drove.

"I know you're not back to using again. Tish?" Patricia sighed.

"Your sister needs wings to fly, baby," she said, bursting into laughter.

"You need to keep your feet firmly on the ground, Tish. And you know what? I don't wanna hear that mess. You had me sitting outside, waiting for you while you went into God knows where to get God knows what. Anything could've happened to me sitting out here by myself, as well as to you being somewhere you shouldn't be."

"Please, I was watching you out the window, your ass was okay."

"Mama was right about you. You're so selfish, always thinking about what *you* want," Patrcia huffed.

"Now don't start that crap with me. There is not one inch of truth in what you just said."

"Out of everybody I know, I thought you were the one who knew me the best. You don't have any reason for this. You don't realize how blessed you are, there's a lot of people who wish they were in your shoes."

"Pat, you don't understand, I'm not as strong as you think I am. I always worry so much about my girls and Darien leaving us. How was I going to take care of myself and the girls with no job training, no husband, and them without a father? I can't do it."

"But Tish, he's not going anywhere."

"I told you that he could now, if he wanted to."

"What went down with you and Darien? I know something happened."

"Nothing. He was sitting at the bar with Tonya."

"He what?" Patricia gasped, shocked.

"You heard me," Tish sighed. "I don't want to talk about it."

As she drove past Khalif's house, she looked up at his window.

That's where she really wanted to be right now. She was anticipating getting back to the house to see if she could catch a glimpse of him through the glass.

Chapter 11

Tish and Patricia were greeted at the door by the girls. Shakima grabbed her hand and let her into the kitchen.

"Mommy, can we make cookies before bed for a snack? You see, we have everything all laid out and ready to mix. We were just waiting on you."

"Oh yes, ma'am. I could use some sweet chewy chocolate chip cookies right about now." Rahanna grabbed her mother's other hand and led Tish over to the table.

"Alright girls, let me wash my hands first. I'll be with you in a minute."

Tish went into the bathroom. She washed her hands, dried them, and was about to leave out the bathroom when she heard Darien's voice. He was not alone; Dutch was with him. Tish pressed her ear to the bathroom door, listening to the conversation between Darien, Dutch and Patricia.

"Well, obviously, there's something going on that she's not telling us," said Patricia.

Tish stayed at the bathroom door, listening a little longer before she decided to walk into her bedroom. She sat down on the edge of the bed, staring down at her shoes, thinking about whether she should interrupt him or not. She was about to get up when Darien walked into the bedroom.

"Dutch and I are gonna go over to the lounge, we have something to take care of," Darien when it to his top drawer, pulled something out, put it in his back pocket, and left out the room.

"Where do you think you're going?" asked Tish. "What did you just put in your pocket?"

"I told you I'm going to the lounge. My wife and her sister have been disrespected and me and Dutch are going to take care of him. It's just a little extra protection, just in case something goes wrong. I have to protect myself."

"I don't think that's a good idea, Darien, you're still on probation. I think I took care of it well enough, you really don't have to go. Patricia and I shouldn't have any more problems out of him." She was following him down the hall towards the living room. He wasn't really listening.

He motioned for Dutch to follow him. Dutch got up off the sofa, "You ready, man?"

"Yes, come on, let's go."

Tish pleaded with Darien not to leave out the door. She told him to think about the girl, think about his future. Darien wasn't paying her any mind as he shut the door. Tish started dialing his phone, but she got no answer.

"Come on Patricia, we have to intervene. We cannot let this happen."

"Darien said he would take care of it. Let the men handle it, they have to do what they have to do."

"You know what? You stay here with the girls, I'll be back," Tish huffed, gathering her stuff.

"No, you cannot go out there by yourself," Patricia put a hand on her sister's shoulder.

"If you're not coming with me, that's exactly what I'm gonna do. I'll call you when I get there."

Tish set off on foot. She walked all the way to the lounge, but by the time she got there, Darien and Dutch were gone. She searched everywhere for them before she started worrying. She began to ask people in the lounge if they had seen them.

One guy told her that all three of them left the lounge, but he wasn't sure where they were going.

"All three of them?" she asked.

"Yeah, I really didn't know the other guy that was with them, but they all left together. It didn't look good either."

Tish left there with only one thing left for her to do: go home and wait. After trying his phone several times she gave up, she started a slow walk back to the house. She made a stop and picked up a little something to calm her down and before she reached her block, she thought about Khalif.

The thought of asking Khalif to ride her around to look for Darien entered her mind, and before she knew it, she was in front of his house walking up the steps.

He answered the door right away, inviting her in. She explained everything to him, but he was not comfortable with going to look for Darien. He didn't want to get involved with that. Khalif explained that to Tish, and she understood. They sat there talking for a while. Tish, starting to feel a little woozy, leaned back on the sofa.

"Why would he dare do something like this when he's still on probation? He's not thinking rationally. I told him Patricia and I handled it."

"I hear what you're saying, Tish, but you have to understand this coming from a man's perspective. There was nothing else left for him to do but go out there and get that man straight. If he didn't, he would've spent too much time worrying about what might happen if you and your sister run into him again."

"You're right," Tish sighed, rubbing her forehead.

"I know I am." He passed her a glass of wine and put her feet up on the ottoman. "Just relax here a little while. By the time you get back home, Darien will be there."

Khalid got up from the sofa and put on some soft music, lit a candle, and sat back down next to Tish. When he looked at her, her eyes were lowering like she was about to go to sleep. He didn't say anything, just letting her doze a little. He didn't see any harm in letting her calm her nerves by getting a little sleep.

30 minutes later Tish opened her eyes and jumped up, looking around. She saw Khalif standing by the window.

"What time is it?" she groaned. "I fell asleep, oh no, I have to get home. I left Patricia with the girls."

"It's only been 30 minutes, Tish. You needed that rest."

"Khalif, no I don't have time for that. Why did you let me do that? Darien should be home by now."

"Tish, you'll be okay, stop worrying so much. The girls are fine, Patricia is fine, you need to think about yourself for a while. What does Tish want, what does Tish need?"

She started to feel a little better, softening her voice a little. "Thank you so much. For being a friend, and for understanding me. Sometimes you make me feel like a teenager all over again, just by being around you."

He sat down on the sofa beside her, lend over and kissed her on the cheek. When he tried it again, she turned her lips around towards him and kissed him back. She opened her eyes and reached up to touch his face as they passionately kissed before giving each other a hug.

"I don't know what made me do that," Khalif sighed, "but I'm glad I did."

"It's okay, Khalif," she said with a smile. "I wanted it just as much as you. Come on, walk me to the door."

They both got up off the sofa. When they reached the door, they got locked back into passionate kissing. This time, though, Tish hesitated and wanted to stop. She broke away from him and told him she had to leave.

"Why, Tish?" he begged. "You know, this is real, what we're both feeling. I want to take it further, and I know you do too."

"I can't, Khalif. I told you that," she says. "That's the problem with you, you don't listen. I'm leaving."

She reached for the doorknob, opened the door, and started running down the stairs. "Call me Tish, as soon as you get home," Khalif called after her.

"I will, good night!"

Patricia was on her way to the lounge, having waited at the house long enough. She knew if she called Tish's phone, she should've acted up trying to get her to stay home. So, she just left.

She looked all over the lounge, not seeing anybody she recognized. She was on her way back with a car pulled up beside her.

"Tish" the man called out. "Tish, Are you okay? Do you need a ride?"

Patricia looked inside the car, "I'm not Tish, I'm Patricia, her sister."

The man's jaw dropped as he could not believe how much she looked like Tish.

"I'm looking for her now, she should have been home. I saw her not too long ago. That's why I thought you were her. I'm John, by the way. How about you come with me, we can look for her together."

Patricia was skeptical, but her worry for her sister outweighed any caution. She got in the passenger seat and leaned against the leather.

What kind of car is this? she thought to herself. As they drove on, she began to get nervous, her actions catching up to her. She had a bad feeling in the pit of her stomach and wanted to get out, *now.*

"If you don't turn this car around, or let me out, you are going to be in a world of trouble." Patricia started banging on the glass, trying to get the attention of a car passing by. She had no luck. The car just kept going. John sped up a little faster.

Patricia tried to grab the wheel to turn it. He reached over and elbowed her in the side of her face, her head hitting the glass. Her vision went dark as she passed out.

Chapter 12

Tish felt really bad about leaving Patricia at home. She hurried as fast as she could to get back to the house. Once she arrived, she walked up the stairs quietly thinking the girls would be asleep. Tish was surprised to see them both up when she entered the house.

"Why are you girls up this time of night?"

"Mama, Aunt Pat hasn't returned yet, she told us to wait up for her."

"Where did she go?"

"She went looking for you, and she's been gone for a very long time."

Tish did not feel up to it at all, but she knew she had to go back out there in those streets to look for her sister.

"Mama, can we go with you, please? We don't want you out there alone."

"No baby, I have to go alone, you girls are going to slow me down. Plus, it's too late for you to be up anyway. Stay here and wait for your dad to come home, tell him I went to go look for Patricia. I'll be right back."

Tish hurried out the door and down the street, looking everywhere. She went by the bar, asking around to see if anybody had seen Patricia. She walked up and down the street where the barber was located, but she came up empty-handed. She started worrying as she headed back home, thinking of Khalif. Before she knew it, she was standing in front of his house. She looked up at the window and saw that the light was still on in the living room, so she went up and knocked on his door.

"Hold up just a minute."

After a few minutes she heard the chain unfastening. Khalif opened the door and was puzzled to see Tish standing there.

"This time of night, girl, are you okay?" he asked.

"No, I'm not okay. I can't find my sister. I've looked everywhere."

"What do you mean? You can't find her? Weren't you all together this evening?"

"Yes, we were, Khalif, but when I came by here, she went looking for me."

"Oh no, you've got to be kidding me."

"I wish I was. Please, you have to help me find her."

"You won't have to ask me twice, I'll come with you. Let me lock up the house." They both headed downstairs.

The first thing they did was go back to the bar to ask more questions and give people descriptions. They walked in and out of a few of the neighborhood stores but had no luck at all.

"How could this happen? I don't understand it. This is a whole grown woman that's lost. This is not happening."

"Baby, she will turn up. Maybe she ran into someone she knows."

"No, the chances of that are very slim. She's not from here."

"You go home Tish, just in case she shows up. I'll stay out here. I'll walk back-and-forth around your house and around the bar, I'll call you if I see her."

"I guess you're right. no sense in me making myself sick over this. I won't be any good for anybody." Khalif walked to her door, giving her a peck on the cheek. She smiled.

"Don't worry, baby. She's going to be okay. I'll call you soon." She just smiled at him and walked into the house.

Tish woke up the next morning on the sofa. She had gotten out the bed in the middle of the night, leaving Darien to sleep on the couch, praying for Patricia to walk through the front door. But as she watched the sun rise up and bright, she knew Patricia was still out there. She had the worst feeling in her stomach.

"I got to call mama," she mumbled to herself. "I have to let her know that I couldn't find Patricia."

She dreaded picking up the phone, but she knew that it was something she had to do. She dialed the number, hung the phone up, and dialed it again. The phone rang three times before she got an answer.

"Good morning, mom."

"Tish? Is that you? Wow, it's good to hear your voice."

"I have some bad news, Mom, are you sitting down?"

"Yes, I am. I'm actually having my morning coffee, what's going on?"

"It's Patricia, Ma. She left out last night and didn't come back."

"You mean to tell me she stayed out all night?"

"Yes, she did. She was actually out there looking for me."

"Why was she looking for you?"

"Mom, I just went out for a little while. I had no idea she would do that. I wasn't gone that long. I'm going to call around some places today before I go to the police department, I'll keep you informed."

"Okay, baby, call me if you hear anything. I'm sure everything is okay."

"Mom, has she ever done anything like this before?"

Yeah, actually, she had stayed over at a few friends' house without letting me know. I didn't hear from her until the next day, but I know all her friends and trust them. I wasn't worried about her."

"Alright mom, I'll call you later on today."

"Alright baby, I'll be praying."

"Thank you, mom." Tish hung up before calling Khalif.

"Hey baby, I was about to call you. I was talking to a few people in your neighborhood, and they were telling me about a man that some of the women were having problems with. Some of them had to send him to jail a few times. They gave me an address, it may be nothing, but I think it's worth checking out."

"Yes, I think so too."

"Tish, this man is a known pedophile. He could have her there with him right now. I'll meet you in about 20 minutes in front of your house."

They hung the phone up. Tish looked at the girls, they were still asleep having also been worrying about Patricia all night. She noticed that Darien was asleep as well but decided against waking him.

Khalif and Tish walked up to a gate that was old, worn, and about to fall apart. Khalif opened the gate and walked up on the porch. Tish was behind him looking around the ground for footprints.

The house was painted gray but looked very worn with many cracks. The paint was peeling and there were leaves everywhere.

Khalif walked up the squeaky steps and up to the door. As soon as he touched the doorknob it creaked open. They both covered their nose because of the foul stench that soon followed.

The colonial style furniture was very dusty, looking like something out of an 1800s film. Old table and chairs colored dark green, heavy suede curtains up to the windows.

"Oh God Khalif, what is that?"

"What is what?" He looked to see what Tish was pointing at. A dead cat, all dried up and still intact, laid on the ground. The smell of death made Tish want to turn and run, but her heart felt that her sister was near, and she had to continue.

Tish followed Khalif to every room, she didn't want to be left alone. There was only one more room to check before they were sure that Patricia was not there. Tish felt relief and wanted to leave.

The house gave her an uneasy creepy feeling. She was also getting tired of holding her breath because of the awful smells.

"Oh no, no, no," Khalif repeated heartbroken and in disbelief, quickly turning to stop Tish from coming in. She fought him still because she knew it was Patricia and knew she was gone.

"Please Khalif, just let me see her!" she begged, pulling at his shirt, trying hard to pass him.

"I'm not gonna let you see her like that, Tish. She's gone, baby, let's get out of here."

"Are you crazy?!" she yelled. "I'm not leaving here without my sister! I'm not. Let me see her Khalif!"

"Believe me, baby, you don't wanna see her like this." Khalif had trouble catching his breath while bent over holding his stomach. Tish had punched him in the gut so hard he had to let her go.

He had to rush over quickly to catch her from falling as the sight was too much to bear.

Chapter 13

A FEW HOURS EARLIER

Patricia breathed in the awful stench of the dead cats as she gasped for air. The plastic bag was wet from breathing and was tied to her head for what felt like days.

She felt a dull paint in her chest from the heavy rope tied around it. Other ropes were tied so tightly around her ankles she couldn't feel her feet anymore. Everything was blurry from the wetness of her eyes. She let out a loud scream while desperately trying to feel the floor.

"HELP! HELP! SOMEBODY PLEASE HELP ME!!" she yelled as loud as she could. "IS ANYONE THERE?"

She cried out, but there was no answer. The wood chair she was tied to squeaked with every movement. Patrica knew it was an old chair; she thought if she kept working, she could break it up enough to get loose.

She wiggled front to back and side to side continuously until she finally fell to the floor with three legs still attached.

Patricia laid on the cold damp floor until she caught her breath. Again, she tried to work on the other chair legs. Once she was free from the chair, she crawled on both knees and she made her way over the wall, banging on it as hard as she could.

I'm quite sure everyone thinks I'm dead by now. I don't even know how many days I've been gone. Where is the man who tied me up like this, and what does he want with me? Where am I?

All I remember is walking towards Khalif's house, looking for Tish. A man called me by her name from his car window and I assured him that I wasn't her, and that I was looking for her. I hesitated before getting in his car, he looked so trusting and seemed to know a lot about Tish.

It was less than three minutes sitting in his car when I began to feel uneasy. He had suddenly stopped talking like he was in deep thought or something, and now it was me with all the questions.

I suddenly had the feeling that I had just made the worst mistake of my life, fear flooded my mind and I immediately started searching for the locks.

"What are you doing?" He had asked me.

"I think I'll just walk the rest of the way," I replied. He laughed out loud and turned down the radio

"Do you want to see your sister or not... you can trust me. I wouldn't do anything to hurt you. I know Tish and Darien very well."

"You know where she is?"

"Of course I do, I took her there."

After that, all I can remember is seeing his elbow raise up towards me. Then, I blacked out

Chapter 14

Ambulances and police cars surrounded the house. Tish went wild when she saw the four paramedics carrying a body out through the crowd. They laid the body on the stretcher.

She covered her sister's body with her own, holding on tight. As Patricias's wrist dropped from the movement, so did the bracelet. A man's bracelet. Tish was sure recognized it and tried hard to remember who it belonged to. She was the only one who saw it and now it was a clue as to who did this...

Khalif talked to the police while she made her way back to the car.

At the police station Tish sat back, still examining the bracelet. It was then that she remembered. It all came back to her. It had to be the same bracelet; the same one John had on the last time she saw him.

She called Khalif over to where she was sitting.

“What’s that in in your hand” he asked.

She quickly put her finger up to her lips, “Shhh!”

She looked around to see if anyone was looking. “We have to get out of here,” she said in desperation. “Where’s your brother”

“He’s locked up...”

“For what?”

“Child support...”

“Oh, never mind, we need to make up an excuse to leave here now.”

“Where are we going, Tish?”

“Trust me Khalif, please.”

“Okay, but your mom and daughter just walked in, so maybe deal with that first.”

Tish put the only clue and evidence she had into her front jeans pocket as she made her way through the crowd of police and detectives to confront her mother and daughter. She put her arms around them both.

“What happened, Tish? What happened to my baby?”

“I’m sorry mom, she’s gone,” Tish choked up, barely able to get the words out. “We found her an hour ago.” Her mom screamed and yelled to see her.

“No mom, please, you don’t wanna do that. There’s nothing there to see, momma, you will not recognize her.”

As her daughter stood there hanging onto Tish’s every word she asked, “Is she in heaven now, Mom?”

"Yes baby, she's in heaven resting now. Don't worry, okay?"

"Mom, are you okay?"

"Yes, I am." As the tears rolled down Tish's eyes, she grabbed her daughter and held her tight. "Where's your sister?"

"She asleep."

Tish called over Darien, who was still talking to the detective, "I have to go."

"Go where, Tish?"

"I'll be right, look after them until I return." Darien watched as Tish and Khalif walked out the door.

Sometimes, I think I should walk away from all this, Khalif thought to himself. *But I how much Tish needs my help, and I could never do that to her and live with myself.*

The funeral was quick, most of her friends from her hometown couldn't make it. Tish said a few words and Darien got up to speak as well about the times he and Tish had together with Patricia. Shakima asked if she could sing, and Tish felt it was okay if she could handle it. Dutch helped the other men carry Patricia's casket. They all gathered in a circle around the casket once it was lowered into the ground. They prayed and dropped their flowers onto the wood.

As they drove out of the cemetery Tish leaned her head against the passenger window.

She was in deep thought about the last conversation she and Patricia had. The sun was shining brightly. It was a little windy, but Tish rolled the window down to feel the air pressure against her face. She looked down at the obituary that she was holding in her hand, then looked back up again. It was then that caught a glimpse of a man standing at the corner of the cemetery, just looking towards the graves. As the car drove past him, she noticed he looked familiar to her, which gave her an eerie feeling. She looked at Darien, who was driving and had his eyes straight on the road.

"Darien, did you see that guy standing by the cemetery? He looks familiar, where do we know him from?"

"I'm sorry, I didn't see anyone. I'm driving."

"I know you're driving, but you're looking from side to side. You didn't see anybody standing there?"

"No, I didn't."

"Circle around the corner, I'm quite sure I know this guy from somewhere."

"I don't have time for this, I want to get home and take these clothes off. It's been a long day," Darien groaned.

"Please, you have to circle back. There's something about him."

"Alright, if you insist." He quickly turned the corner and went all the way around to the front of the cemetery, but there was no one there. The man was gone. "Okay, so that was about nine minutes out of our day wasted."

"Darien, please." Tish took the bracelet out of her purse and looked at it. The image of the man came to her as soon as she touched, it was the first person she thought about. "Take Mom and the girls home, there's something that I need to do.

"What is it that you have to do, Tish?"

"I need to check something out. It's very important. Let me out here. I'll see you at the house later, is your phone charged up?" she asked. He checked his phone quickly.

"I have 50%. I'll put it on the charger once I get home."

"Okay, I'll call you if anything comes up."

"Look, you be careful. I tell you if it's not one thing, it's another with you, Tish." She got out of the car and walked to the back, opening the back door to give the girls a hug. She told her mom that she'd see her later.

"Okay baby, you be safe."

"There's food at the house, just warm it up and I'll see you guys later. I love you so much."

Her mother and daughters exchanged their goodbye while Darian just looked at her and turned his head. After they drove off Tish just stood there for a while, looking at the bracelet. She pulled her phone out to call Khalif. He picked up right away, "Hey baby, everything okay? I'm sorry I couldn't make it to the funeral."

"That's alright, I understand. Something just came to me, and I need you to go back to the house with me."

"You're talking about the house where Patricia was found?"

"Yes, that house."

"Why would you want to go there?"

"Because there's something about this bracelet. I believe if I go back there, I'll figure everything out. There's just so much going on with me right now, I can't put things together."

"Where are you, Tish?"

"I'm on the corner of Central Avenue and 12th St."

"I'll be there in a minute"

When they entered the house Tish started going through the dresser and kitchen drawers. looking for names or pictures. Someone had come and cleaned the house up; they must be getting ready to put it on the market.

"I don't know who would want to buy this rundown house, it's awful."

Tish picked up a piece of paper, "Look, this looks like an electric bill. See the name, I know that name. This is the name of our old landlord."

"Are you sure?"

"Yes, I'm positive. This is him," she took the bracelet out of her pocket. "And he was wearing this bracelet. I also saw him at the cemetery today. Khalif, we must go to the police department now. I know who did this."

"Oh my God, you've got to be kidding me. Baby, you're a genius. Come on, let's go." They stormed into the police department. She was looking for the sheriff who took care of them the other day. As soon as she saw him, she almost knocked him down. He regained his composure.

"What is it? What's up with you now"

"I know this sounds crazy, but this bracelet belongs to an old landlord of mine. I saw him pick this bracelet up from trash and put it on."

The sheriff turned to Khalif, "Sir, could you get her out of here? I don't have time for this. I mean, a bracelet? Come on now."

"No, you have to listen to me. Something is not right with this guy." She showed him the electric bill that she found in the drawer. "This is him, he lives in this house. I know he did."

Her phone rang. She sighed, answering it, "Hello Darien."

"Where are you, Tish?"

"I'm at the police department right now. You remember the guy who we rented the apartment from? He lived in the house where we found Patricia. He owned it or something, I don't know, but the bracelet that Patricia had in her hand belonged to him."

"So, you're saying that he's the one who did this to Pat?"

"It's a possibility. Something's wrong with that guy, he's off. He's always acted weird to me Darien." Tish paused when she heard a voice in the background. "Who's there? Who's that I hear in the background?"

"That's my sister and her girlfriend, they stopped by to pay their respects. They thought the reception was going to be here. Once they left the burial grounds and didn't see us, they came straight here."

"Okay, I'll be there shortly. And you know I do *not* want her in my house, around my children and my mother. You know that. Get her out of there as soon as you can."

"You don't have to be like that, Tish, it's all good. I'll talk to you in a little while." She hung the phone up. She told the police officer some more about John, they felt that it was a good idea to check the story out. They sent a car over to the house that came up on his profile, it was a different address from where they found Patricia.

"Listen, you go home, and we will call you after we question him. We don't want you around here when we bring him in."

"Please, just keep me informed." They brought John down to the police department and questioned him. Around the same time, Tish was walking into her house to confront Darien and who she suspects to be his lover. But when she walked in, the house was quiet. Her mama was laying on the couch. She walked through the hall, looking into the girls' room.

Shakima was asleep and Rahanna was reading. "Mom is everything okay?"

"Yes baby, everything is good. Where's your dad?"

"Him and Dutch left."

"Was there anybody else with them?"

"Oh yes, there was a nice lady. Her name is Tonya, we talked for a little while and she's also interested in art, just like I am. She's really nice, mom, is she one of your friends?"

"No, she's not. She's your aunt's friend. Do you know where your dad went?"

"He didn't say, he just said he'd be back."

"Alright, if you need anything let me know. Did you all have enough to eat?"

"Yes, we did. We saved you some also."

"I'm not hungry, baby. I'll get something later on, maybe." Tish went into the bathroom and got her things together for a shower. After her shower, she went to her bedroom, which was in disarray from her not being home that much. she took off the bath towel and put on her pajamas.

She called Darian but he didn't answer. She dialed back again and left a message, "Call me as soon as you can. The police are on their way to pick up John for questioning."

She then called Khalif, "Man, can you believe my husband had his lover in my house, around my kids and my mother This is not going down like that. He must have lost his mind. They were gone when I came home, but it doesn't matter, she shouldn't have been in here at all. I just don't understand why she has to be intertwined into my family, like they don't know what's going on. Everybody knows that they are messing around. Why is he bringing her around me like that?"

"She just wanted to pay respect to your sister, I don't see nothing wrong with that."

"I think it's very disrespectful."

Khalif sighed, "Baby, get some rest. Call me as soon as the police department finishes with the investigation. When they contact you, I'll take you down there if you want me to."

"Okay I'm about to get some sleep. Listen, I know this is the guy. He used to get fresh with me when I was pregnant with my first daughter, he always gave me this uneasy feeling when tried to come on to me. I never even told Darien about that."

"Well, I hope this is the guy so we can finally put this behind us. We'll talk soon, I love you." All of a sudden it was silent; Tish was shocked to hear that.

"I'll call you as soon as I hear something, Khalif." She hung up the phone. Three hours later, Darien walked through the door. The sound of voices coming from the living room woke her up.

He was talking to her mother, "I guess she's asleep. I'm gonna go take me a shower."

"Alright son-in-law."

"You know mama, you can stay here as long as you want to. You're welcome to move in if you want to."

"Baby, I've got a whole life waiting for me back home. My plants, my friends, I have a full life. I'll be alright." Tish just laid in the bed, listening to Darien run the shower, humming to himself, wondering where he was coming from and how long was he with his sister's friend.

When Darien was finished with his shower he came into the room. Trying not to make a sound, he put his clothes into the hamper. Tish just laid there with her eyes open. Darien took his robe off and got in the bed. Tish waited for about 30 minutes, and when she heard him snoring, she got out the bed and took his clothes out of the hamper. Then she went into the bathroom and started smelling his clothing around the neck of his shorts, his T-shirt, and his underwear. Her suspicion was right, she smelled perfume and sex.

She stormed back into the bedroom and turned the light on. "Darien, wake up. Wake the hell up! This is what I'm talking about, you bring your shit into my house, that is so disrespectful. I'm not taking this from you no more. I'm going through too much right now. Why would you do this?"

He was trying to wake up out of a deep sleep, "Tish, what?" She threw the clothes at him.

"This is what I know you've been doing." He turned over and covered his head. Tish pulled the whole blanket off of him and threw it to the floor. Darien jumped up, grabbed her, and threw her to the bed.

"This is crazy. You're gonna stop this mess and you gonna stop it now. I told you there's nothing going on between us. In fact, I will call her right now and have her tell you that nothing is going on."

"You're not gonna do a damn thing, she can't tell me anything. You've given me so many reasons to doubt you, Darien. I don't feel like this is a marriage anymore. I know what the hell sex smells like, and cheap dollar store perfume. I smelt the same perfume at the funeral parlor when she and your sister came over near me. I smelt it then and it's what I'm smelling right now. Just come out and tell me the truth."

"Okay, okay," he let her go, picked the blanket up, and got back in the bed, covering himself.

"Okay what? Are you gonna tell me the truth of what's going on between you two? Are you going to tell me what I already know?"

"I didn't mean for it to happen like this-" She stormed out of the room, sitting down on the chair in the living room. Her mother looked up at her, having heard the entire conversation.

"Baby, you've got a decision to make."

"Yes mama, I know I do. I'm not the one to get in between marriage, and you know I love Darien, but I'm telling you, that girl needs to get away from him. I don't like how she moves, mama."

"I understand, I know exactly what you're talking about."

"I've been feeling it for a long time, but he got me out of a mess. He helped me get my life back together. He was always a good husband to me. I just felt like I was never good enough for him."

“Sometimes people grow apart from each other, it’s not guaranteed that that person will always be in your life. Sometimes you have to move on. But you must try, not just for you, but for the girls as well. Get some counseling.”

“You’re right mama,” Tish sighed. “I’m tired, I’m just gonna lay here and doze off. I’m waiting for the police officer to call me with some news about Patricia’s murderer.”

“Okay baby, I hope you and Darien can work out your problems.”

Around 7 AM Tish awakens to the sound of her cell phone ringing, it’s the police department.”

“Miss Tish, we need you to come down to the police department right away.”

“I’m on my way,” She hangs up. “Darien! We have to go down to the police department!” Darien jumped up, threw his clothes on quickly and ran into the bathroom to wash his face before running out the door. Darien was speeding but Tish told him to slow down.

“Look, I want to live, I have a life to live for, unlike you.”

“Why you say that?”

“Because you put everything in jeopardy. You’ve jeopardized your marriage and your family playing house with Tonya.”

“We’ve been friends for a long time, I just can’t break off a friendship like that.”

“Darien, I know better than that. I know you’re more than friends. We’ve been together 15 years, 12 years of marriage, and you think I don’t know you by now? You were slipping away from me before you were incarcerated. I knew something was going on.”

"So what? You wanted me to sit up under you every night? I wasn't gonna do that."

"I'm not saying that you have to do that, but you have a family, and you never act it."

"It is what it is, I'm tired of talking about it."

"I am too."

There was nothing but silence until they got to the police department The police officer looked at Tish, "Ma'am, I'm sorry for your loss. We at the police department just want to extend our condolences. We know what you are going through at this moment. We just need you to answer some questions."

They took her to the back, into a small room. "Do you want anything to drink?"

"No, I'm okay," Tish shook her head. They pulled out a chair for her.

"So let me ask you, you have stated that when you went over to your sister while she was in the stretcher, you opened the bag-"

"No, the bag was already open. I just looked inside, and I saw this in her hand. I just reached down and grabbed it without anyone seeing it. I had never seen this bracelet before, it was something new to me, but then I remembered where I saw it before."

"And you're saying that it was your old landlord?"

"Yes, yes, my husband went to him to collect our security deposit, and I was supposed to meet him there, but when I arrived, he was already gone." She looked at Darien to confirm that she wasn't going to tell the police officer why he was already gone. "I saw him pick his bracelet up from the trash and put it on his arm. This man is not right. He got fresh with me a couple of times."

Darien looked at her.

"Yes, I never told you, I didn't want you to do anything that would mess us up from having a roof over our head. I handled it, baby."

"I'm sorry you had to go through that, Miss Tish, we just need you to sign this affidavit right here, and you can be on your way."

"So, you're sure it's him.?"

"Yes, we have sufficient evidence that he's our guy. We'll keep you informed of the court procedures."

"Alright, thank you so much." Tish didn't want to go back to the house with Darien. She wanted to go see Khalif, to tell him what just went down. *It was about time for this mess to come to a head. I refuse to play the victim anymore, and no one thinks about me. I was only staying until that situation was over, and that horrible smell on his clothes told me enough. I'm not ready to go home yet.*

"Let's go to your sister's house," Tish said,

"For what?"

"No special reason. I just want to go by there, do you have a problem with that?"

"Oh man, here we go. Alright, if that's what you wanna do." Tish got a text. Darien looked down at her phone. "Who is that?"

"It's Khalif, he probably wants to know what happened."

"Yeah, that's something we need to talk about too."

Tish laughed, "There is nothing at all to talk about, trust me. It's nothing compared to what we're discussing now."

When they pulled up Darien got out of the car and walked around to the other side to open the door for Tish. And as she suspected, Tonya was right there, obviously waiting on Darien. She raised on eyebrow when she saw Tish, "I didn't know you had someone with you. Come on into the living room."

They all sat in the living room together, not saying a word. She just watched for reactions as Regina walked in.

"Hey brother," his sister began. "How did it go at the police department?"

"Well, we found the right person, now he has to go through a trial. They're gonna keep us informed, but I just feel so bad the way everything went down. She didn't deserve that, not at all."

"You're right, she did not deserve that."

Tish sat up, "How would you know what she deserved, you didn't know her at all. You did not know my sister."

"You're right, but we knew of her, through Darien," Tonya jumped in. "We've been talking a lot, especially about our future."

"About your what?"

"You didn't tell her, Darien? You told me you were going to tell her." Tonya looked at Darien.

"Tell me what?" Tish stood up from the sofa.

"I tried to tell you last night, things are just not working out for us."

"It's not working out because of variable you threw into the equation, that's why it's not working out. I wanna know how long you two have been messing around behind my back. Obviously, it had to have been before you were incarcerated, which I always had a feeling about."

"I think our marriage has just come to an end."

"I'm confused, why did you come home to me? Why didn't you just go straight to Tonya?"

"I had to find out how you really felt first."

"I've heard enough I don't need to hear no more," Tish turned and walked out of the living room, telling Tonya goodbye and before leaving through the front door.

Darien ran behind her, "I'm gonna take you home."

"No, you're not gonna take me home. I don't need you to. Goodbye Darien." He tried to convince her to get in the car, but she refused. People were gathering as they were making a scene now, so Darian backed off and let her walk away. Tish found herself in the arms of Khalif, crying as he consoled her. He explained to her that this has to stop, and she had to get her life together and back on track.

"You're grieving your sister," he started, "you're grieving a marriage, you're about to lose a new job, you have to think about the girls. They need you now more than ever. So, you go home and talk with them, be with them. Don't worry about me. I'll be here for you whenever you need me."

"I believe you will." Tish hugged him and headed out the door to be with the girls. When she got home, she noticed noise coming from the bedroom. She walked in and saw Darien packing. "Okay, so you're doing what you always wanted to do."

"No, this is not what I always wanted to do, you're forcing me to do this. I can't take the pressure anymore, and I don't have to"

"So where are you going to go? Your sister's?"

"No, I'm gonna stay in a hotel for a while and just think things over." Tish didn't say anything else to him. She just let him continue packing. She sat in the living room with her mother and watched him leave out the front door. In a way, she felt some kind of relief. She didn't want to be in that marriage anymore. She finally ran into somebody who she really cares about her, somebody she could have a future with, to build with, and to be there for her, and Darien was not the one for that. Now, it seems like he moved on to just doing things that he wanted to do, things that would satisfy him.

Two weeks later, Khalif and Tish were sitting in the restaurant having dinner when Khalif got up, bent down on one knee, and presented Tish with an engagement ring. He looked her in the eyes, "Tish, I want to spend the rest of my life with you. I want to be with you and the girls and my son and raise them as our children. I don't want this with anybody but you, so I'm asking for your hand in marriage."

His eyes were wide, and he was shaking very nervously. She looked at him and said, "I don't want to be anything else but your wife, Khalif. It's made me so happy to know that you can give us the foundation that we need."

TO BE CONTINUED...

Milton Keynes UK
Ingram Content Group UK Ltd.
UKHW040257291024
450401UK00014B/209/J

9 798369 431894